SNUFF TAG 9

SNUFF TAG

A Nicholas Colt *Thriller*

JUDE HARDIN

f THOMAS & MERCER

The characters and events portrayed in this book are fictitious. Any similarity to real persons, living or dead, is coincidental and not intended by the author.

Text copyright © 2012 Jude Hardin

Published by Thomas & Mercer
P.O. Box 400818
Las Vegas, NV 89140

ISBN-13: 9781612184470
ISBN-10: 1612184472

For Pat, who has always believed in me.

Chapter One

Dear Mr. Colt: You're dead...

I broke the seal on a bottle of Old Fitzgerald, generously bathed some ice cubes, and took a sip. Satisfied the subject line couldn't possibly be true, I opened the e-mail.

It was spam, an advertisement from a company called Plots with a Twist. They were trying to sell me a hole to be buried in and a high-tech grave marker—a solar-powered, weatherproofed video screen embedded in a slab of granite. When your loved ones walked up and pressed a button, they got to watch all the good times you had when you weren't a stiff yet.

I decided not to get one. When I kick, I want to be jettisoned into outer space, like the guy who played Scotty on *Star Trek*. I always wondered if his publicist set that up, just for the good press. You never know about those Hollywood types.

I finished my drink, closed the laptop, and headed down to the lounge. I had a one o'clock appointment with a guy named Nathan Broadway.

I'd driven to St. Augustine and checked into the Holiday Inn the night before, thinking a couple of days at the beach might be good for my soul. My adopted daughter Brittney was living in one of the dorms at the University of Florida in Gainesville, and my wife, Juliet, and I had been separated for some time. Juliet was living near Jacksonville, in the house we once shared, and I was back in my 1964 Airstream Safari travel trailer on lot 23 at Joe's Fish Camp. It got lonely out there sometimes. I missed my daughter, and I missed my wife.

At 1:05, Nathan Broadway still hadn't shown up. I took a seat at the bar.

It was Sunday, October 9, and the Jacksonville Jaguars were playing the Cincinnati Bengals on the big-screen television. There was a free buffet table set up against the back wall. Pigs in blankets, fried cheese, potato chips, and a bunch of other greasy, salty fare designed to make you hang around and buy more six-dollar beers. A dozen people stood in line, waiting to cram as much food as possible on paper plates slightly larger than drink coasters. Near the front of the queue a tall woman in a business suit kept rubbing her nose with a handkerchief. When she sneezed in the general direction of the hot wings, I decided I wasn't hungry.

"What can I get you to drink?" The bartender's name tag said Sheri. She had a long blonde ponytail I guessed to be fake and a gold stud in her tongue I guessed to be genuine. Nice smile.

"Old Fitz on the rocks," I said.

She made the drink and I started a tab. Jacksonville scored a touchdown on their opening drive. While they were getting set to kick the extra point, Nathan Broadway walked in and sat on the stool next to mine. He ordered an Amstel Light and said, "Mind if we move to a booth?"

I shrugged, got up, and followed him to the table farthest from the television. A few people cheered when Jacksonville made the extra point. It was seven to nothing. Nathan Broadway and I sat facing each other. I guessed him to be in his early thirties. He wore a crew cut and jeans and an orange polo. Clean-shaven, looked like he went to the gym. He pulled an envelope out of his back pocket and handed it to me. There was a letter inside, typed on a single sheet of white paper, and a hand-drawn map.

Dear Nathan Broadway: You are cordially invited to come and play a game called Snuff Tag 9. We have provided a map for your convenience. You will need a vehicle with four-wheel drive to get there. Come alone. Pack as you would if you were going to stay at a hotel overnight. We will be expecting you on October 11 at approximately 8:00 p.m. If you choose not to come, you will die. If you try to trace this letter, or try to get the authorities involved in any way, you will die. If you show this letter to another living soul, you will die. This is not a joke. We will kill you. Thank you for your cooperation, and we look forward to seeing you on the 11th. Sincerely, The Sexy Bastards.

I looked at the envelope. No return address, no postmark, no stamp.

I laughed. "Snuff Tag Nine. Sounds like some kind of second-rate action movie."

"You're kidding, right?" Broadway said. "It's one of the most popular video games on the planet."

"I don't play that shit," I said. "So I wouldn't know."

"It's really cool. Violent as hell. You can play alone or you can go online and play against other people. I've even played against people in foreign countries. I signed up for a tournament a while back, so maybe that's where these sexy bastard people got my address. I don't know."

"You found the letter in your mailbox?" I said.

"Yesterday. I opened it and, I don't know, it scared the hell out of me. I thought about calling the police, but I was afraid whoever put the letter in my mailbox might find out and really kill me. I thought it would be safer to call a private eye. I appreciate you meeting me on a Sunday, Mr. Colt, on such short notice."

I took a sip of my drink. "How many other private investigators did you call?"

"Only two."

I tried my best to look crushed. "So I wasn't your first choice?"

"You were third in the phone book."

"Must have been an old phone book."

"What do you mean?" he said.

"I mean it must have been an old phone book. I'm not a private investigator anymore."

He looked confused. "What are you, then?"

"I'm nothing. I don't have any sort of license anymore. Long story. If it makes you feel better to call me something, call me a security consultant."

"I thought I was going to be dealing with a licensed professional. Now I'm not sure. I mean—"

"I was a licensed investigator for a long time," I said. "I know what I'm doing. And apparently I'm the best you're going to get on a Sunday on short notice."

He nodded. Took a swallow of beer and wiped his mouth with the cocktail napkin he'd brought from the bar. "OK, so what should I do? You think someone is really aiming to kill me? They said it's not a joke."

"They said that, but it probably is a joke. These kinds of letters make the rounds from time to time. If it was me, I would wad it up and throw it in the trash can."

He fidgeted with the napkin, twisting it into a skinny rope. "I don't know. I don't want to take any chances. I don't like threats, you know? I mean, I can take care of myself, but—"

"So what do you want me to do?" I said. "There's no way to trace the letter. We could take it to a laboratory for fingerprints and DNA, try to find the sender that way, but it would be expensive as hell and I doubt anything would show up. I imagine whoever handled the letter and the envelope used gloves. The way I see it, you have three choices: you can ignore it, which is what I would recommend; or you can rent a jeep and follow the directions on the map and find out for yourself that it's only a prank; or you can hire me for a hundred dollars an hour, plus expenses, and I'll drive out there for you and report back that it's only a prank."

"A hundred an hour?"

"Yeah, and the clock started ticking at one."

"So I owe you fifty bucks just for sitting here and talking?"

I looked at my watch. "That's about right. So what's it going to be?"

He stared at his mutilated cocktail napkin for thirty seconds or so, and then said, "How about we ride out there together?"

"Nope. I don't take clients on jobs with me. If I go, I go alone. I'll need a thousand-dollar retainer up front. If there's any left over, I'll refund the difference."

He reached into his pocket and pulled out a checkbook.

"I'll need cash," I said.

"Where am I supposed to get a thousand dollars cash on a Sunday?"

"At the front desk. I already asked, and they said it shouldn't be a problem."

"How will I even know you went out there to check it out? You're so convinced it's a hoax, you could just—"

"I'll take pictures and e-mail them to you from the site. That good enough, sweetie pie?"

He studied the label on his beer bottle, ignoring my sarcasm.

He was starting to piss me off. When you hire a private investigator, or a former private investigator who lost his license over a narcotics conviction and now calls himself a security consultant, or any professional, there's a level of trust involved. If you don't trust them to do the job you want done, don't hire them. Simple. Broadway had gone down the alphabetical list in the phone book. That had been the extent of his research. Going down the alphabetical list in the phone book is a stupid way to hire a chimney sweep or a house painter or a guy to pump out your septic tank.

Never mind someone you think might save your life. But Nathan Broadway's stupidity was his problem, not mine. I needed the work, and if he wanted to fork over a thousand bucks to send me on what I figured would almost certainly amount to a wild goose chase, then I wasn't above taking it.

"Can I at least see your driver's license?" he said.

I took it out of my wallet and handed it to him. He glanced at the surgical scars on my left hand but didn't say anything.

"Satisfied?" I said. "I have references too if you need them. All you have to do is ask."

"That's OK. It's just a lot of money, that's all."

He took a deep breath, looked over at the television for a second, and then wrote the check. We walked to the front desk together, and the cash went from his hand to mine.

Chapter Two

I told Broadway I would be in touch. We shook hands and he left the hotel.

I went back to my room and did some searches on the computer, but I didn't find any organization called The Sexy Bastards. Snuff Tag 9 was a different story. I got over a million hits on Google. I clicked on the Wikipedia article and skimmed through it. The premise seemed simple enough: There are 999 characters, and you get to choose which one you want to be. Once you choose, seven others are randomly assigned as opponents, and at some point during the game a ninth character is dropped into the fray. You and your opponents are given two weapons each from the "secret vault." The secret vault contains ten different weapons: a length of tow chain, a slingshot, a survival knife, a nightstick, a set of brass knuckles, a pair of nunchucks, a stun gun, a can of Mace, a bull-whip, and a fifty-caliber blowgun with three darts. You choose the weapons blindly, so you don't know what you're going to get, and the weapons you select are automatically replaced, so it's possible for other characters to have one or both of the same weapons you have. Your only objective is to kill the other eight characters. If you kill them all, game over. You win. If one of them kills you, game over. You lose. A master of ceremonies named *Freeze* orchestrates the battles and keeps everyone in line.

Freeze is actually a billionaire sadist who has kidnapped the characters and is forcing them to play the game. That's the story line. The characters are being forced to play the game against their will. If you refuse, you die automatically. The playing field is a remote island two miles in diameter, so there's no chance of running away.

The premise reminded me of a story I read in junior high called "The Most Dangerous Game" by Richard Connell. The folks who developed Snuff Tag 9 even mentioned that story as one of their inspirations.

But Snuff Tag 9 was way more complex.

According to Wikipedia, there are twenty different levels of difficulty to choose from based on your proficiency at the game, level twenty being the highest. As of the date on the article, only four people in the world had ever won the game at level nineteen, and nobody had ever won at level twenty. Nobody even knew what level twenty looked like, except the programmers. Rumor had it your final battle in level twenty was against Freeze himself, but nobody knew for sure. The article said Snuff Tag 9 was listed as one of the top ten most violent video games ever produced and was rated M for mature players only.

I poured myself another drink and sat there for a while and thought about it. Someone had taken the time and trouble and risk to hand-deliver a letter and map to Nathan Broadway's mailbox, just to lure him to a remote location to play a video game. The whole death threat thing was bullshit, I was sure of it, but maybe the note had an underlying sinister purpose written between the lines.

I called Broadway's cell phone number.

"I forgot to ask earlier, but what kind of work do you do?"

"I'm an accountant," he said.

"Make good money?"

"I do all right."

"You have a nice house? Nice car? Nice things?"

"Mr. Colt, I—"

"And you're single," I said. "Listen, I want you to stay at home Tuesday night."

"Why?"

"I'm thinking whoever put that letter in your mailbox is planning to burglarize your house. All that Snuff Tag Nine crap was just to make sure you were away for a few hours after dark. That's my guess, anyway. There was a similar case down in Tampa a few years ago, only in that one the letter told the recipients they'd won a seven-day cruise. The targets were single people. Educated. Affluent. All they had to do was show up at a certain time and place to collect their prize, but the address they'd been given turned out to be a vacant lot. While they were gone, the crooks waltzed in and bagged their cash and jewelry and laptops, anything of value that could be carted out easily."

"Were the thieves ever caught?" Broadway said.

"Not to my knowledge. Hell, it might be the same ring."

"So you think I should stay home Tuesday night? What if they come anyway? Should I buy a gun?"

"When they see your car in the driveway and lights on in the house, they'll go somewhere else. I guarantee it. They probably cased a dozen houses and delivered a dozen of those letters, maybe more. The people that fall for it are the ones they'll hit. Do you have a dog?"

"No."

"An alarm system?"

"No."

"Professional burglars look for those things and target residences that don't have them. Just stay home Tuesday night and you'll be fine."

"You sure?" he said.

"Yeah, but you might want to think about having an alarm system installed sometime soon."

"I will. I sure will. Are you still going to drive to the spot on the map?"

I hesitated. "I'll go out there, just to check it out. But I would lay odds there's nothing there. Shouldn't take more than four hours tops, so I'll be giving you back quite a bit of the retainer."

"Wow, that's great. I appreciate it, man."

"No problem. I'll give you a call Tuesday night."

We disconnected. It was going on three o'clock, and I still hadn't eaten lunch. Come to think of it, I hadn't eaten breakfast either. I had a three-bourbon buzz and didn't think it would be wise to drive, so I locked the room and walked out to the beach and headed toward the pier.

A mile or so south and two blocks west there was a bar and grill called The Oasis. I'd been there before, and the fish sandwich was consistently good and reasonably priced and the draft beer was ice cold. I took my Topsiders off and trudged through the loose sand until I got to the firmer part by the shore. From there I put the shoes back on and treaded easily. There were people throwing Frisbees and playing volleyball and surfing and jogging and walking their dogs. It was low tide, sunny, and eighty degrees. People up north get the leaves changing and frost on the pumpkin and all that, but to me this was the perfect autumn day.

Perfect, that is, if I'd had someone to share it with.

Eighteen months after an overwhelmingly traumatic time in Tennessee and California, where I was brainwashed by a Christian militia group called the Harvest Angels and used for some shockingly abominable activities, my wife Juliet still hadn't found it in her heart to forgive me for one night with a record company receptionist named Ericka. I explained to her a million times that I wasn't myself at the time, that it was meaningless, but there was something about the Filipino culture she'd been brought up in that made it very difficult to work through marital infidelity, even in extreme circumstances like mine. I kept telling myself she just needed more time, and I sincerely hoped that was the case.

I made it to The Oasis, and a hostess carrying a stack of laminated menus ushered me to a table upstairs. I sat there and pretended to look at the lists of appetizers, soups, salads, and entrees, and when the waitress came I ordered a fried fish on rye and a Heineken draft.

She brought the beer, and while I was waiting for the sandwich my cell phone pulsed and the caller ID said Brittney. I answered.

"Hi, sweetheart."

"Hey, Daddy. You'll never guess what just happened."

From the sound of her voice I knew it wasn't bad news. "What?" I said.

"I won tickets to the Florida-Georgia game in a raffle. Isn't that just awesome? I'm going to the game!"

"Wow, that is great. When is it?"

"October twenty-ninth at three thirty. It's in Jacksonville, at Everbank Stadium, where the Jags play. You want to go?"

Truth be known, I didn't care that much about college football. Even the Florida-Georgia game, the biggest event of the season in this part of the country. But, like the credit card commercial would say: *An afternoon with your daughter—priceless.*

"I would love to go," I said. "I can't believe you're asking me instead of one of your friends."

"Actually, I have four tickets, so I can invite a couple of friends too. Oh, we're going to have such a great time. I can't wait! So where are you?"

"Just hanging out at the beach."

"Where at?"

"St. Augustine. Want to drive over and have some dinner with me later?"

"That sounds so good. But I have a calculus test tomorrow, so I better stay here and study. Are you working in St. Augustine or taking a vacation?"

"A little bit of both. I'm going fishing in the morning, and I'll probably stay here tomorrow night, but I have a job up near the Georgia border Tuesday."

"It's nothing dangerous, is it?"

"No. Nothing dangerous."

"You should totally get back into music and let someone else spy on cheating husbands and stuff."

"I can't play anymore," I said. "You know that."

"But you can still sing."

I didn't feel like talking about it.

"Have you ever played a video game called Snuff Tag Nine?" I said.

"I haven't, but I know some guys who play it. I've watched them. It's like really graphic ultraviolent stalking kind of stuff. Lots of killing, lots of gore. Why, you getting into video games now, Dad? Thinking about joining the twenty-first century?"

"No, just curious. If you change your mind about dinner, just give me a call. OK?"

"OK. I will. Daddy, I'm so excited about going to the game."

"I can tell. Me too. Talk to you soon, sweetheart."

"Bye, Daddy. Love you."

"I love you too," I said.

My grouper sandwich came, and I ate it and ordered another beer and then I walked back to the hotel.

chapter Three

Early Monday morning, before the sun came up, I met Joe Crawford at the Cat's Paw Marina and we boarded a fifty-foot charter boat called *Sea Love III*. The boat was licensed to carry thirty-four passengers, but I counted only a dozen people in line ahead of us and four behind us. Slow day. We left the marina and headed for the open sea at six thirty, as scheduled.

I'd known Joe Crawford since we were twelve, since sixth grade. In a life where friends and acquaintances came and went, Joe was a constant. He was my best friend and I loved him like a brother. Like the brother I never had. He ran the fish camp on Lake Barkley where my Airstream was parked, so he was also my landlord. He gave me a discount for helping with security around the place, and he let me use one of his rental boats whenever I wanted. Joe owned the fish camp, and he also dabbled in international real estate. He was rich, and he'd offered me full-time employment more than once, but full-time employment wasn't my thing. I also didn't want the possibility of a working relationship putting a strain on our personal relationship.

"Beautiful morning," Joe said.

We were leaning against the steel railing atop the starboard bulkhead. Cruising at around fifteen knots into a pink and turquoise and gold sunrise over the Atlantic.

"It is," I said. "We picked a good day to go out. Perfect. We got lucky."

"I've been looking at buying a boat myself, maybe even living on it part of the time. It's something I've always wanted to do. Nothing as big as this, of course, but maybe a thirty-five-foot Jersey or something."

"Sure. You could call it the SS *Minnow*, and I could be your bumbling first mate."

He laughed. "Seriously. I could see myself cruising up and down the coast, docking in Puerto Rico for a week or two. Or the Bahamas. I could see myself living like that."

"If it's something you've always wanted to do, then do it. It's not like we're getting any younger. I was thinking about doing the same thing, back when I had lots of money like you."

"Come to work for me," he said. "I can show you how to make lots of money again."

"It's not me, Joe. You know that. I'll probably be doing this private eye thing till I drop. I'll never get rich, but at least I'm living life on my own terms."

"I know you're not married to it, though. You were back to playing music full time before all that crap in Tennessee."

I fingered the scars on my left hand. "Yeah."

"Just think about it, OK?"

"OK. I'll think about it. But really, business has been pretty good lately."

"Anything interesting?"

"The usual, mostly. Bogus insurance claims, cheating spouses, a skip-trace here and there. Yesterday a guy hired me because of a letter he got telling him he had to show up at a certain place. The letter said he had to show up and play a video game called

Snuff Tag Nine, and if he didn't The Sexy Bastards were going to kill him."

Joe looked at me and we both started laughing.

"Snuff Tag Nine?" Joe said. "The Sexy Bastards?"

"Yeah. What a crock of shit. I'm thinking it's a burglary ring, sending these letters out to get people away from their houses. I'm going to check it out and then probably hand it over to the sheriff's department."

"Why don't you just hand it over to the sheriff's department now?"

"Guy wants to pay me a hundred an hour to check it out, I'll check it out. I'll check it out all day every day for a hundred an hour."

"Can't blame you there," Joe said. He looked at his watch. "I'm going below to get some coffee. You want some?"

"Sounds great."

"Be right back."

There were two guys standing a few feet aft of us, leaning on the same steel rail on the same starboard bulkhead. One of them followed Joe to the lower deck, and one of them stayed put. The guy who stayed put didn't say anything to me, and I didn't say anything to him. I'm not much for striking up conversations with strangers, and apparently he wasn't either. Joe came back with the coffee a few minutes later. He and the guy who'd followed him down were saying something to each other. Joe's different from me in that way. He can strike up a conversation with anyone, at any time. The guy handed his friend a cup of coffee, and Joe handed me one. The two guys walked farther aft and then out of sight.

"See," Joe said. "You never know when the opportunity might arise to make some money. I was in line to get the coffee and a guy started talking fishing with me. Eventually he asked me what I did for a living. I told him, and he asked for a business card, and

I gave him one. Turns out he's an investor, looking to buy some property in Canada."

"You're good at stuff like that," I said. "Wheeling and dealing off the cuff with someone you just met. Me, not so much."

"You've hustled guys on the pool table before, haven't you?"

"Not as good as you have."

"See, looking me in the eyes and saying that is a hustle in itself. It's the same thing in business. You say things that make the other guy feel good about himself. Once you do that, he's on your side."

"But there's an art to it," I said. "If you're obvious, the guy's going to know you're a phony and walk away. Some people have a knack for that sort of thing. It's a talent, like playing guitar. I made a fortune playing guitar, and you made one being full of shit."

Joe sipped his coffee. "All right, my friend. Whatever you say. I still think you could be a hell of a salesman if you wanted to."

I tried to imagine myself in a suit and tie and shiny black shoes that hurt my feet. I was still trying to imagine all that when the engine slowed and the crew came around with tackle and coolers full of bait. Time to stop thinking and do some fishing.

Chapter Four

Tuesday evening I drove to the destination on the Snuff Tag 9 map, a spot deep inside the Okefenokee Swamp on the Florida side. My 1996 GMC Jimmy had four-wheel drive, but it turned out I didn't need it. The washboarded dirt road that led to the site happened to be dry on October 11, and anyone with a Honda Civic and a kidney belt could have made it in with no problem.

I switched off the ignition, opened the windows, and listened. A crow cawed and a hornet buzzed by and a raccoon or squirrel or fox or something rustled some leaves in the nearby woods, but mostly I heard what you would expect to hear out in the middle of nowhere: nothing.

Nothing bothers me. It bothers my tinnitus, a condition that causes ringing of the ears. I attribute this condition to years of playing the guitar on some of the world's biggest stages, fifty thousand watts of power blasting through walls of speaker cabinets taller than some houses.

In the mid to late eighties my southern rock and blues band, Colt .45, consistently sold out sports arenas all over the country. Gold records, mansions on both coasts, garages full of high-end automobiles. All of that came to a screeching halt the day I crawled away from the fiery wreckage of a chartered jet. The crash took the lives of my wife, Susan, and my baby daughter, Harmony, and all the members of my band. I was the sole survivor. Twenty years later, I found out the crash wasn't an accident. I found out Susan and Harmony died because of their skin color. The white supremacist pieces of shit responsible for the incident called everyone else aboard collateral damage. I was supposed to have died, but I didn't. I walked away without a scratch. The sound of silence always makes my ears ring and it always makes me think about the people I loved whose lives were wasted.

I looked at my watch. 7:08. I had gotten to the Okefenokee early so I could take some photographs of the site before dark and send them to Nathan Broadway as promised. I planned to stick around till eight, just to make sure the Snuff Tag 9 letter was indeed a bogus subterfuge. In the highly unlikely event that it was not, I had my favorite carry revolver holstered under the tails of my Hawaiian shirt and a sawed-off twelve-gauge pump strapped to the back of the Jimmy's front passenger seat.

I sprayed on some mosquito repellent, took my camera out of its case, and got out to snap a few pictures. The cypress trees surrounding the clearing were heavily draped with Spanish moss, and some of them had purple carnivorous pitcher plants clustered at their bases. The sun was setting and the full moon rising and the area took on an eerie glow I knew the camera wouldn't capture.

An owl hooted in the distance. I followed the sound and tried to zoom in on it with my telephoto lens, but the bird was well camouflaged and it took me a while to find it. I scanned the treetops for several minutes and finally saw a big yellow eye peering back at me. I snapped the shot. The eye was huge. You could have served a piece of pie on it.

I heard some splashes, so I knew there was some water nearby. Probably a gator having dinner, I thought. I didn't follow the sound and try to zoom in on it with my telephoto lens. Alligators don't amuse me. I hate them. When I was fourteen, a friend from school named Randy Osborn invited me to stay the night one time. We were goofing around one of the water hazards at the golf course across the street from his house when a gator came from nowhere and bit his right arm off at the elbow. I knew a little first aid, enough to tie a tourniquet and keep him from bleeding to death. Randy didn't show up for school the next week, or the week after that. Or the week after that. I never saw him at school again, but I saw him in my dreams for a long time. Alligators don't amuse me. I hate them.

The owl hooted again. It was getting spooky out there in the swamp. It was creepy as hell, and I started feeling like the guy who always gets slaughtered at the beginning of a horror movie. I climbed back into the car and put the camera away and rolled up the windows.

Before I'd left civilization, I'd stopped at McDonald's and bought two Big Macs and a large coffee and a bottle of spring water. I drank the coffee on the drive to the swamp, and I figured the burgers would give me something to do while I waited for eight o'clock. I unrolled the top of the bag and opened one of the Big Mac boxes and took a couple of bites and washed it down with some water.

When we were still on good terms, Juliet used to fuss at me every time I bought fast food. She's a nurse and she sees people younger than me admitted to the hospital all the time with heart attacks and strokes and other health issues brought on by life-times of bad choices. I knew she had a point, but I had given up cigarettes over three years ago and still attended Narcotics Anonymous meetings over the heroin addiction I'd acquired while imprisoned by the Harvest Angels. I'd always been kind of skinny and my blood pressure and cholesterol stayed within normal limits, so I didn't think the occasional cheeseburger or scoop of ice cream was going to kill me.

Thinking about Juliet made me want to call her. I looked at my cell phone, but there was no signal. I was too deep in the wilderness, too far from a tower. I made a mental note to call her on the way home. I opened the second Big Mac box and thought about it and decided one was enough. I stuffed the empty box from the first burger and the empty coffee cup and some dirty napkins into the McDonald's bag and rolled the top of the bag tight and set it on the passenger's-side floorboard to throw away later.

By 7:55 the sun was gone all the way but the moon was bright and I could still see the shapes of the trees and the Spanish moss. At 8:03 I decided nobody was coming. I reached for the ignition switch and something hit the windshield with a thud and then rolled off the hood and fell to the ground. I pulled my flashlight out of the glove box and my revolver out of its holster and opened the door and got out, thinking maybe the owl I'd heard earlier had accidentally smashed into the glass. I walked around the car and pointed the light at the object by the front tire on the passenger's side.

It wasn't an owl.

It was Nathan Broadway's head.

chapter Five

My throat got tight and my chest felt like a bare-knuckle boxer was in there trying to beat his way out. I looked around and didn't see anybody, but a few seconds later electric lights from high in the trees flooded the clearing with blinding brightness. A male voice from an amplified speaker said, "Drop your weapon, Mr. Colt."

"What the fuck?" I said. I wondered how he knew my name.

"Drop it or die. Last chance."

If Nathan Broadway's lifeless gray eyes hadn't been staring up at me, I might have made a move for the shotgun. But these guys obviously weren't screwing around. I tossed the .38 a few feet in front of me and raised my hands.

"You win," I said. "Who are you? What do you want?"

"We wanted Mr. Broadway to come here at eight o'clock, alone, like our letter to him unequivocally specified. Apparently he didn't take us seriously. At least not seriously enough. Too bad."

Broadway had taken the note seriously enough, but I had talked him—and myself—into thinking it was a ruse to jack some valuables from his house. I felt somewhat responsible for his untimely demise, and things weren't looking real rosy for me at the moment either.

The voice told me to get on the ground and lace my fingers behind my head. I did that, and a minute or so later someone put a knee on my back and cuffed my hands and blindfolded me. I heard my revolver's hammer being cocked back, and then I heard the cylinder being rotated. He had picked up my gun and was checking to see how many cartridges were in there. It had a full load of six. I heard him ease the hammer back and stuff the gun somewhere in his pants, either in his pocket or his waistband.

"Get up."

I stood. "Since you know my name," I said, "it seems only fair that I should know yours."

He didn't say anything. His breath smelled like pipe tobacco. He strapped what felt like a leather dog collar around my neck and started pulling me forward with a leash.

"You sound like a Greg," I said. "Is it OK if I call you Greg?"

"Shut the fuck up."

We walked a few yards and then I heard another set of footsteps fall in behind me. We crunched through the woods and made a series of disorienting turns, and after a few minutes a car door opened and the guy behind me put his sweaty hand on the back of my neck and guided me into the backseat. The interior of the vehicle smelled like leather conditioner and Armor All, with just a hint of the aromatic tobacco I'd smelled on Greg's breath.

Something hard went down on the center console.

"That his gun?" Sweaty Hands said.

"Yeah. Stick it in the glove box for me."

I heard the glove compartment open and then close.

"You guys mind telling me where we're going?" I said, just to be saying something. I knew they weren't going to tell me. I wondered why they hadn't killed me already. The engine roared to life and the vehicle lurched forward.

"What should we do with him?" Greg said.

"Up to you," the other guy said. I decided the other guy sounded like a Jim. "Of course we're a man short now, so we could—"

"He's too old. We'll have to find someone else."

"Just a thought."

We were on a highway now, the tires humming at cruising speed. I'd noticed the height of the vehicle when I'd climbed in, and with the way it handled and the leather seats and everything I figured it to be a Cadillac Escalade or one of the other expensive brands of four-wheel-drive sports utility vehicles that normally never go anywhere more adventurous than the mall. They hadn't forced me to lie on the floorboard or anything, so I guessed the windows were tinted darkly enough that a cop or a trucker or an ordinary concerned citizen wouldn't notice the blindfolded prisoner in the backseat.

Greg had said I was too old for something. I wondered what.

"I'm only forty-nine," I said. "You guys need someone for your softball team or something? I'm an excellent pitcher. No kidding."

"Can I just shoot him now?" Jim said.

"I don't want to mess the car up. We'll wait and see what Freeze wants to do."

Damn. My fate was in the hands of a video game character. For some reason I didn't find much comfort in that.

Chapter Six

The car stopped and the door opened and Greg said, "Get out."

I didn't move.

We'd been on the road for an hour or so, and during that time I kept thinking about Rule #16 in Nicholas Colt's *Philosophy of Life*: Never go down without a fight.

The *when*, *where*, and *why* of this situation were still a mystery, but there was no doubt in my mind about the *who* and the *what*. Greg and Jim were going to kill me. They'd killed Nathan Broadway, and they were going to kill me. It was only a matter of time. Maybe it would be in ten seconds, or ten minutes, or ten hours, but it was going to happen. I still had the use of my legs at the moment, so I figured now would be the best time to at least take one of them with me.

When Greg reached in and impatiently grabbed my leash, I reared and swiveled and kicked both his kneecaps with both my heels. I only grazed the right one, but I connected solidly with the left. I felt it give and heard the ligament snap. It snapped like a dry twig. While Greg was falling to the ground and shouting *motherfucker*, I quickly rolled onto my back and wriggled my legs through the loop of my cuffed hands. Now the cuffs were in front. I pulled the blindfold off. Jim was reaching for the glove compartment, and he had it open and had his hand on my .38, but before he got his finger on the trigger, I got the handcuff chain around his neck and gave it a quick jerk. His face turned blue, and he fell toward the console wheezing and clutching his throat.

I stretched between the front bucket seats and grabbed the revolver. I looked back in the cargo area and saw their weapons, a deer rifle and a shotgun. It would have been nice to have had the firepower, but there was no way for me to handle either of the big guns with my hands cuffed. I figured I could handle the big SUV with no problem. It wasn't a Cadillac Escalade. It was a Mercedes-Benz G-Class. Silver with a black leather interior. It had tinted windows. I'd gotten that part right. I scooted to my left and exited the door Greg had opened for me. We were parked in a horseshoe-shaped driveway in front of a very large house. It was a mansion, a sprawling estate you would expect a movie star or pop singer to live in. Greg was lying on his back with a cell phone to his ear, tears streaming down his face from the excruciating pain I'd inflicted on what used to be his left knee.

I pointed the .38 at his head and said, "Give me the keys, bitch."

"You're dead, motherfucker."

I cocked the hammer back. "Reach into your pocket, slowly, and pull the keys out and toss them to your right."

He reached into his pocket, slowly, pulled out a can of Mace, and sprayed it directly into my eyes.

I squeezed the trigger, but nothing happened. I squeezed it again and again and again, but the gun did not fire. Greg must have dumped the bullets back at the swamp. The world was a blur and my eyes felt like someone had jammed acid-dipped razor blades into them. A few seconds later someone grabbed my leash and I felt two sets of hands grip both my arms. I was being led toward the house, and I had no choice but to follow.

"He's too filthy to take inside," one of the guys said. "Let's hose him down."

"Fuck that. Let's throw him in the goddamn pool, see if he can swim with the cuffs on."

"Freeze wants him alive."

Freeze wanted me alive. At least I had that going for me. I still couldn't see. I heard the click of a knife blade lock into place, and one of them started cutting my shirt while another undid my pants. They forced me to the ground and yanked my shoes and socks and jeans and underwear off, and the next thing I felt was the stinging cold spray of a garden hose.

"Stand him up."

They stood me up and rinsed me off some more with the icy water. My eyes had started to clear some and I could see the guy with the hose. He looked to be about the same age as Greg and Jim and was dressed in the same kind of durable outdoor clothing. He wore dark-rimmed glasses and a gold watch, and his blond hair was parted neatly in the middle.

"That's enough," a voice from behind me said.

Two of them patted me down with towels and then they led me naked through a set of French doors on the side of the house. The doors led to what looked to be a very large and fancy gardening shed, with rakes and shovels and wheelbarrows and weed eaters and every other tool you could think of hanging immaculately on pegboard walls. There was a workbench and a vise against one wall and a wire dog kennel against another. The kennel was empty. It was huge, meant for a Saint Bernard or a Great Pyrenees or one of the other giant breeds.

It didn't take me long to realize it was meant for me.

Chapter Seven

They forced me into the cage and secured the door with a pad-lock. Someone had bolted wheels onto the corners, which raised the kennel several inches from the floor and allowed it to be moved easily with an occupant inside. The steel wire was very uncomfortable against my naked skin. There was a plastic jug full of water and one that was empty. I assumed the empty one was for me to pee in. The cage smelled like bleach, as though it had recently been disinfected.

The guy who'd been operating the hose reached into his pocket and pulled out a cell phone. He put it to his ear and said, "Hey." He listened for a few seconds and then responded with, "All right."

"What's up?" one of the other guys said.

"Freeze wants him in the theater in five minutes."

"Should we put some clothes on him?"

"Fuck it."

They wheeled me through an interior set of French doors and down a short hallway to an elevator. One of the guys pushed the button, and the elevator went up and we got out on the first floor, which looked more like the lobby of a fancy hotel than someone's house. There were tall plants and paintings and leather armchairs and a fish tank. "You've Got a Friend" played softly from invisible speakers. The Carole King version.

We turned a couple of corners and entered a large auditorium with a raised platform on the end farthest from the door. There were multicolored lights attached to overhead steel trusses, and at the center of the platform there was a man sitting in a high-back chair. He was sitting there like it was his throne. I assumed the man in the chair was the one they called Freeze. The lighting was such that I couldn't make out the features on his face, but he looked to be bald and tall and enormously fat. Behind him were two large video screens.

"Leave us alone," the fat man on the stage said. His voice was high-pitched and effeminate. It didn't match his size.

The guys who had wheeled me in left and closed the doors behind them.

"Nice place you got here," I said. "But I really should be going now."

"Allow me to introduce myself. My name is Freeze."

"Is it *Mister* Freeze, like on *Batman*?"

"It's just Freeze. Like Prince is just Prince and Madonna is just Madonna. And you're not going anywhere. You're here because you fucked up my game."

"Sorry about that, bubba. So tell me, are the gorillas who threw me into this cage The Sexy Bastards? Because to tell you the truth, I didn't find them all that attractive."

"You'll never know who The Sexy Bastards are. Nobody will ever know."

Big fucking deal, I thought. But it did make me curious.

"People are going to be looking for me, Freeze. When they find me—"

"They'll never find you. The life you had before you were contacted by Nathan Broadway is over now, Mr. Colt. I just haven't quite decided what to do with you yet."

"How do you know my name?"

"I'll show you in a little while. It didn't take a lot of research to find out all about you once I had a name. There's a nice Wikipedia article. Did you know that? I know all about you and your band and the plane crash back in the eighties, and I know you've been working as a private investigator for the past fifteen years or so. What I don't know about are those scars on your left hand. Maybe you could fill me in."

"Maybe you could kiss my ass."

He laughed. "You're a tough guy. I like that. You really did a number on my guys who drove you here. Impressive. That's why I think I'm going to give you a chance."

"What are you talking about?"

"I'm going to put you in the game. I'm going to let you play Snuff Tag Nine. You'll be taking Mr. Broadway's spot."

"You motherfuckers hosed me down and put me in a cage like an animal. What makes you think I'm going to play any crazy goddamn video game?"

"Oh, you'll play. You'll play, or you'll die. Those are the only two choices in Snuff Tag Nine. You see, I've taken the premise of the video game, only I'm playing with real people. It's much more fun that way. Allow me to explain. Tomorrow morning, an AICD, an automatic implantable cardioverter defibrillator, will be surgically implanted into your chest, just below the left collarbone. These devices are typically used for people with bad hearts, to convert life-threatening rhythms back to normal. The device you'll be getting, however, has been somewhat modified. The device you'll be getting will, on remote-controlled command, convert your normal cardiac rhythm to a deadly one called ventricular fibrillation. That's V-fib for short. If at any point you refuse to play the game, your heart will be forced into V-fib and you will collapse and die. If at any point you break any of the rules of Snuff Tag Nine, your heart will be forced into V-fib and you will collapse and die. If at any point you attempt to go beyond the boundaries of the playing field—"

"OK, I get the picture." I couldn't believe my ears. This son of a bitch was insane. Literally off his fucking rocker. "So what happens if I agree to play your little game?" I said.

"You'll probably die anyway, but you'll at least have a chance. Here's how it works: you and seven other contestants will be taken to what we call the field. The field is actually an undeveloped area in the Okefenokee, several miles from where you were earlier. It's all private property and all fenced in. You'll be given some survival gear, some food and water, and two weapons. The object of the game is to kill all the other players. It's very simple. The last man standing wins."

"I thought the playing field was supposed to be an island," I said.

"On the video game it's an island, and I could have bought one easily enough, but it just wasn't practical. For one thing, there's really no such thing as an uncharted island anymore. They're all marked on maps, and I was afraid activity on one might show up in some satellite photos or a passing ship might see smoke from a fire or something. The risk was too high. Plus, electric power was going to be a big problem. My land in the swamp is much more practical than an island, and it's too far from anything we would call civilization to worry about anyone bothering us out there. It's the perfect place to play the game. It takes place over five days and, like I said, the last man standing wins."

"And then what?"

"And then you're set for life. I'm a billionaire, Mr. Colt. I treat my winners like kings. Of course I can't allow them to go back to their former lives, but they're treated like kings nonetheless.

They're taken overseas and given new identities. They're given everything they want."

"Sounds great. How do you keep them quiet?"

"The AICD you'll be getting in the morning will be permanent. If you win, you'll be monitored closely for the rest of your life. If you ever mention the game to another living soul, your heart will be forced into V-fib and you will collapse and die."

"What about deathbed confessions? Sooner or later—"

"That'll never happen. Over forty-five thousand people in the United States disappear every year. Without a trace, as they say. Nine of those people play Snuff Tag Nine. Some of the others are family members of Snuff Tag Nine players, players who decided not to cooperate in one way or another. Do the names Juliet and Brittney mean anything to you?"

He had me. The son of a bitch had me, and he knew it.

Chapter Eight

The video screen on Freeze's left blinked to life. "I'm going to introduce you to the other players," he said. "But first, I want to show you this."

The stage lights went down, making the video screen seem brighter. The guy whose knee I'd broken, the guy I called Greg, was walking to the front door of a nice-looking brick house. He knocked on the door, and Nathan Broadway answered.

"Mr. Broadway?"

"Yes."

Greg reached into his pocket, pulled out a leather badge case, and flipped it open. "I'm Detective Krebs, Jacksonville Sheriff's Office. We're investigating some threatening letters that were sent out a few days ago regarding a game called Snuff Tag Nine. We have reason to believe that some of those letters were delivered to this neighborhood."

"Actually, yes, I got one of those letters," Nathan said.

"May I see it, please?"

Nathan took another look at the badge. "I guess so. Would you like to come in?"

"Well, it would be better if we could talk down at the station. If you wouldn't mind."

"Am I in some kind of trouble?"

"No, no. Nothing like that. My partner and I just need to ask you some questions, and we'd like to use a tape recorder for future reference. If you don't mind, that is."

"I guess that'll be all right. Let me just grab a jacket."

The video cut to a harshly lit interior. There was a concrete floor with oil stains on it and a lawn mower draped with clear plastic and a Ping-Pong table folded up and rolled to the side. It was the inside of a residential garage. Nathan Broadway was sitting in the middle of it, strapped to a wooden chair with duct tape. There was a Japanese samurai sword mounted on the wall several feet behind him. Greg was smoking a cigar. I assumed the other guy, Jim, the guy who had sprayed Mace into my eyes, was doing the camera work.

"Who did you show the letter to?" Greg said.

Nathan was panting. "Nobody," he said.

Greg slapped him hard with the palm of his hand. "Yes, you did, Nathan. You showed the letter to someone. You went to the Holiday Inn at the beach Sunday afternoon, and you had the letter with you. Now think, real hard. What was the person's name you showed the letter to?"

"I didn't show it to anybody."

Greg touched the lit end of the cigar against Nathan's right earlobe. You could hear the sizzle of the fat cooking. Nathan screamed out in agony.

"Give me a name," Greg said.

Nathan was on the verge of passing out. His pulse pounded in his neck. "I swear I didn't show it to anybody."

I figured Nathan was trying to protect himself as much as he was trying to protect me. The letter clearly stated that he would die if he showed it to another living soul. Maybe he thought he still stood a chance if he didn't confess.

Greg grabbed Nathan by the hair and yanked his head back. He held the cigar like a pencil and guided it to within an inch of his left eyeball.

"Give me a fucking name!" he shouted.

Nathan lurched and coughed. It looked like he needed to vomit but couldn't because of the position he was in. "Oh god," he cried. "Not my eye. All right. All right. His name is Colt. Nicholas Colt. He's a private investigator. Please. Oh *god*! Please, I don't want to die. Please don't kill me."

Nathan started bawling like a baby. Greg walked behind him and lifted the sword from its mount. I knew what was coming next. I didn't want to watch, but for some reason I couldn't turn away. Greg gripped the handle of the sword tightly with both hands and stood with it cocked over his shoulder like a baseball bat. He swung hard and fast, and Nathan Broadway's head toppled off his shoulders and rolled across the wooden floor. Broadway's heart was still pumping, even with no signals coming from his brain, and bright red blood from his carotid arteries sprayed and splattered on the low ceiling.

Someone had done some amateurish editing to the film, and the footage of the head rolling across the floor kept playing over and over. They'd added some effects, making the scene look and sound like some kind of perverted bowling alley where Nathan's freshly liberated noggin was the ball.

Finally the screen faded to black.

"Well?" Freeze said. "What did you think?"

"I think you're a sick motherfucker."

"I thought it was great. In fact, I'd like to see it again. Maybe I'll make some popcorn this time. Do you like popcorn, Mr. Colt?"

"Why do you get your jollies watching other people die? What did Nathan Broadway ever do to you? What did *I* ever do to you?"

"Everyone needs a hobby, eh? Mine is Snuff Tag Nine. I invented it. I took the idea from the video game, but I invented the version for real people. Not too many people can say they invented their own sport. And it's much more interesting than football or hockey or anything you can find on ESPN. My players literally fight for their lives."

"I hate to tell you this, Mr. Freeze, but the ancient Romans invented the same goddamn thing. The players were called gladiators. What you're doing here is nothing new. The ancient Romans were some sick motherfuckers, and you're a sick motherfucker, and you're going to fall hard just like they did."

He sighed. "Well, you're wrong about that. Ever heard the expression 'too big to fail'? That's me. I have more money than some countries have, Mr. Colt. I have cars and yachts and jet airplanes and fabulous mansions all over the world. I can have a different sex partner every night if I want, and I'm not talking about some sleazebag prostitute either. I'm talking quality poo poo. But I get bored with all that, you know? It's all just so...ordinary. I need something fresh and new and exciting. Snuff Tag Nine is kind of like the television show *Survivor*, only in my version the contestants play for keeps. Anyway, enough of all that. I said I was going to introduce you to the other players, so on with the show."

Chapter Nine

He pushed a button on his remote and two men appeared, one on each of the screens. The guy on the left wore a jersey with the number *1* printed on the chest, and the guy on the right wore the number *2*. Both jerseys were red. Both men were Caucasian.

"Number One is an insurance salesman from Waterloo, Iowa," Freeze said. "He's six foot one, weighs one hundred and eighty pounds, and holds a second-degree black belt in tae kwon do. He's single, of course. All my contestants are single. Number Two is a computer programmer from Hannibal, Missouri. He got his undergraduate degree from Stanford and played second seed on the tennis team while he was there. He's six feet even, weighs one sixty-five."

"They have names?" I said.

"Their names aren't important. *Your* name isn't important. From now on, you'll be known as Number Eight. It was supposed to have been Nathan Broadway, but now it's you."

He clicked the remote and two more guys popped up on the screens.

"Number Three is a physician, a radiologist from Quincy, Illinois. He's tall, almost six five, and he weighs two hundred and ten pounds. He played basketball in high school and, more recently, soccer in a corporate league. He likes to hunt deer with a bow. Quite good at it. Number Four is an electrical engineer from Indianapolis, Indiana. He's five nine and weighs one seventy. He's a gym rat, pure and simple. He lifts weights and drinks protein shakes and all that. When we captured him, his blood tested positive for steroids. He's aggressive and unpredictable, like a pit bull or something. I expect him to do well in the game."

"How do you expect me to do?" I said.

"I expect you'll be killed the first day."

"Why's that?"

"All the other men are younger than you and in better physical condition. You don't fit the profile for Snuff Tag, not at all. If the circumstances had been different, I never would have chosen you as a player."

"Then why don't you just kill me and find someone else?"

"We have a schedule to keep. Finding another player would take too much time. The game starts on October twenty-sixth and ends five days later on the thirtieth. The finale is always the day before Halloween. I don't want to deviate from that. No, the finale has to be the day before Halloween. I'm afraid I'm stuck with you, Mr.—I mean Number Eight. I'm hoping you'll surprise me and do better than I expect, but I doubt it."

"The finale is a contest between the last two players alive, right?"

"That's correct."

"So how do you know you'll be down to two players by the thirtieth of October?"

"I'll get to that. Let's just say it's all very carefully orchestrated." He clicked the remote again. "Number Five is an architect from Bainbridge, Georgia. He runs marathons and stuff. He's skinny, as you can see, but his endurance is remarkable, both physically and mentally. Number Six is an airline pilot. He got his training in the Marine Corps and was flying jumbo jets from Louisville to Atlanta when we nabbed him. Very smart fellow, Number Six. His IQ is off the chain, like one fifty or something. I wouldn't be surprised to see him at least in the final four. And look at those eyes. Isn't he just gorgeous?"

"Gorgeous," I said. I said it out of the side of my mouth.

Freeze pushed the button on the remote again, but only one photograph appeared this time. It was on the screen to my right.

"This is Number Seven. He's a diving instructor from Palatka, Florida. He's a former Navy SEAL. It was a bitch getting him to cooperate, but I think he's finally settled down now. He's five ten and weighs one sixty. He improvises well, and he knows about a hundred ways to kill a man with his bare hands."

"What about Number Nine?" I said.

"Pardon me?"

"The game's called Snuff Tag Nine. I just assumed there were nine players. You showed me seven, and I'm the eighth. Where's Number Nine?"

"Ah, very astute of you. That's correct, there are nine players, but the ninth is always a surprise. Typically, the ninth contestant is one of the most challenging players to defeat, if not *the* most challenging. Number Nine has been the winner more than once. All of you will meet Number Nine after the game is underway."

"Can't wait," I said.

"I want to show you one more thing, and then I'll have the guys get you some clothes and a nice room for the night."

"You mean I don't have to stay in this cage? I'm going to get clothes and everything?"

"You're a player now, Number Eight, and officially in training. You'll be given the finest accommodations until the game begins. I have a full-time chef here who's an absolute culinary genius, and I will assign you a personal trainer. Nothing to eat after midnight tonight, though, because you have surgery in the morning."

I didn't say anything. This whole goddamn scenario was surreal. It was blowing my mind. I felt as though I'd fallen into some kind of portal, a rabbit hole to hell. Freeze pushed some more buttons on the remote and a guy wearing the number 6 on a red jersey came up on the screen to my left. I assumed he was a player from a previous year. He was outside, somewhere in the thick brush in the swamp, and it was daytime. His sandy blond hair lay in filthy, disheveled clumps, like someone with axle grease on their fingers had tried to pull it out. Black grimy smudges covered his face and arms. There was some kind of collar around his neck. Not a dog collar like Greg and Jim had put on me, but something that appeared to be hard and plastic and high-tech. He walked along a row of trees connected by lengths of plastic tape about four feet from the ground. It resembled crime scene tape, only it was red instead of yellow. He looked around, ducked under the tape, and started sprinting through the trees on the other side. The scene switched to his point of view, one angle and then another, which told me the plastic collar on his neck was equipped with several cameras. He got maybe twenty feet from the taped-off boundary and then stopped and gasped and clutched his chest. He fell to the ground and twitched a few seconds and made some snoring sounds and then lay quiet and still.

"That's what will happen if you try to escape," Freeze said.

Chapter Ten

The guys came and wheeled me to the elevator and took me to the second floor. They let me out of the cage and led me to a steel door with the number 8 stenciled on it and a deadbolt with the twist knob on the outside. One of them opened the door and I walked in alone and the door shut behind me and I heard the deadbolt click to the locked position.

It was a large suite, maybe twenty by thirty, with plush burgundy carpeting and a king-size bed and a leather sofa and a wooden desk and chair. There was a notepad and a ballpoint pen on the desk and a brushed steel reading lamp. It looked like a good place to sit down and write a suicide note. I scanned the area, looking for a way to escape, but steel bars blocked access to the only window, and the air vents on the ceiling were too small to crawl into. I walked into the bathroom and looked through the vanity cabinet and the medicine cabinet, thinking I might be able to find something to use as a weapon, but there was nothing but a disposable razor and a can of shaving cream and a toothbrush and a tube of toothpaste and some soap and shampoo and deodorant and a spool of dental floss. The mirror over the vanity was stainless steel, like the ones they use in jailhouses, so no chance of breaking off a sliver and making a shank.

I shaved and took a shower and dressed in the set of surgical scrubs they'd left on the bed. I sat on the sofa and tried to think of a way out, but there wasn't one. After a while a guy wearing a white uniform opened the door and wheeled a cart in with a dinner tray on it. Another guy stood outside the door with a machine gun. The guy in the white uniform left the cart in the middle of the room and walked away without saying anything and locked the door. There was a salad and a plastic bottle of Perrier and a shiny steel dome covering what I guessed was the entrée. I lifted the dome, and a puff of steam rose from a mound of fettuccine Alfredo. The pasta and sauce had been ladled onto a flimsy paper plate, the kind you see at rescue missions and church picnics. It smelled great and I was starving so I pulled the cart to the sofa and sat down and ate the noodles and the salad with a plastic fork and drank the bottle of mineral water. It was very good. Soon after I finished, the guy in the white uniform returned with his armed escort and took everything away.

There was a thirty-two-inch flat-screen television on a stand against the wall opposite the couch. I found the remote and switched on the television and scanned all the channels but couldn't find a signal. Then I saw a DVD on the shelf below the TV with *Defibrilador Automatico Implantable* written on the case. I took the DVD out of the case and loaded it into the player. The video was all about the thing that was going to be implanted in my chest in the morning, but it was in Spanish. I couldn't understand what they were saying, but the animated footage gave me the gist of how the device was implanted and how it worked.

I didn't want that thing inside me. Once it was in, Freeze could control me for the rest of my life. I didn't want that, but I didn't seem to have a choice. If it had been just me, just my life to worry about, I would have taken the plastic fork from my dinner cart and stabbed the guy in the white uniform in the eye. I would have used the metal cart as a shield, and I would have rushed the guy with the machine gun. He probably would have shot me dead before I got anywhere near him, but assuming I got lucky and somehow wrestled the rifle away from him and crushed his skull with the butt of it, I might have been able to get outside and make a run for the woods. If it had been just me, just my life to worry about, I might have tried something like that.

But it wasn't just me. Freeze knew about my wife and my daughter, and after seeing the Nathan Broadway video there was no doubt in my mind he would make me watch them die if I tried anything.

"Hello, Number Eight."

It was Freeze. His voice was coming from recessed speakers mounted in the ceiling.

"Hello," I said.

"I trust you enjoyed your dinner."

"Yeah, it was swell."

"Andre is such an awesome cook. Did you find the video about the surgery you're having in the morning?"

"I found it, but it's in Spanish."

"Oh, my. That was a mistake. I'll have the English version sent in right away."

"Forget about it. I'm having second thoughts. I've decided not to go ahead with the procedure after all. Tell them to bring me a movie or something instead."

"You're funny, Number Eight. Try to get some rest tonight, OK? Sweet dreams."

"Hey, before you go can I ask you one question?"

"Go ahead."

"Let's say I win the game and you set me up in another country and all. What's going to stop me from ripping that defibrillator thing out of my own chest or hiring someone to take it out for me? What's going to stop me from doing that and coming after you and wringing your fat fucking neck?"

"Such language. You really need to watch that. Anyway, the device you'll be getting has a special tamper-proof circuit. Any attempt to remove it will result in a deadly electrical discharge. Your heart will be forced into V-fib and you will collapse and die. Then your estranged wife and your adopted daughter will be tortured for several days before we finally kill them as well. But you're not going to have to worry about any of that, because you don't have a chance in hell of winning the game. Any more questions?"

"No."

"Good night then, Number Eight. See you bright and early."

Chapter Eleven

They came and got me before sunrise. There were three of them, two wearing surgical greens like mine and the other khaki pants and a sports jacket. The guy wearing the khaki pants and sport jacket was carrying a gun. I could see the bulge under his left sleeve. He looked familiar, but I couldn't put my finger on where I'd seen him before. He stood there and watched while the other two put an IV in my arm and strapped me to a gurney and wheeled me out of the room. We took the elevator to the first floor.

"How long will this take?" I said.

"Less than an hour," one of the guys in scrubs said. "It's a very simple procedure. Don't worry, you'll be fine. Freeze would have our heads if anything ever happened to one of his players."

"Will I be anesthetized?"

"Yes. In fact, I'm going to give you something to help you relax as soon as we get to the operating room."

In the operating room they stripped me naked and transferred me from the gurney to a stainless steel table draped with white absorbent pads. There was a cart beside the table with an assortment of surgical instruments arranged neatly on top and something bundled in a blue towel on the shelf below. They wrapped a blood pressure cuff around my left arm and clipped a wire to my right index finger to monitor the oxygen level in my blood. One of the guys piggybacked a small IV bag onto the larger one, and a couple of minutes later a wave of euphoria washed over me and I felt myself slipping into unconsciousness.

I fought it off.

I couldn't let this happen.

I couldn't let them do this to me.

I rose and ripped the IV out of my arm and tore off the blood pressure cuff. The guy wearing khaki pants and a sports jacket went for his pistol, but before he could get it out of the shoulder holster I snatched a scalpel from the cart beside the operating table and used it to slit his throat ear to ear. His eyes bulged and he clutched at the wound and gurgled and coughed and fell to the floor. I grabbed his gun and shot Green Scrubs One in the chest. Green Scrubs Two ran for the door, but I drilled a round in his left ass cheek before he got his hand on the knob. He fell and retched and I finished him off with two shots to the head on my way out.

I took a right out of the operating room and ran and ran, but I was groggy from the drug they'd given me and my legs felt like there were sandbags tied to them. It was like trying to run underwater. The hallway seemed to go on forever.

I finally made it to a T and had to decide, left or right. I took a left and soon found myself in a large area with dozens of people milling around. The people weren't paying any attention to me, which was odd considering I didn't have any clothes on. Along the perimeter of this large space there were doors with numbers on them, and outside some of the doors there were people sleeping on blankets on the floor. I walked by them, trying to be as quiet as possible, the pistol in my hand as inconspicuous as a shark in a bathtub.

A nurse walked up to me and said, "The doctor will see you now." She wore an old-fashioned form-fitting white dress and white nylons and one of those stiff hats with a red cross on it.

"I'm not sick," I said.

"It's just a checkup."

"All right."

She didn't seem to notice my nakedness. I followed her through one of the doors and into an examining room. She took my blood pressure and temperature and told me to wait there. A few minutes later a bald man wearing wire-rimmed eyeglasses and a stethoscope stalked in and said, "Your blood pressure is too high. We need to operate."

"I feel fine," I said.

"I need you to get on the table now. It won't take long."

I was tired. Someone had hooked lead anchors onto my eyelids and I couldn't keep them open, no matter how hard I struggled. I climbed onto the examining table and reclined to a supine position, and the doctor wiped my chest with something cold and wet. There was a bright light and I felt an uncomfortable pressure, like someone had placed a concrete block on my left collarbone.

"How do you feel?"

"I'm OK," I said. "I don't need an operation."

I heard laughter. I opened my eyes and saw the blurry face of Green Scrubs Two, the guy I'd double-tapped on my way out of the operating room.

"We're all done," he said.

"But you're dead. I shot you."

He laughed. "That's the anesthesia talking. Don't worry, it will wear off shortly. We're going to take you back to your room now."

"You're finished with the procedure?"

"Yes."

"That thing's in my chest now?"

"Everything went fine."

His version of fine and my version of fine were altogether different. In my version, I'd blown his brains out with a nine-millimeter semiautomatic handgun. Everything had seemed so real. I couldn't believe it was only a dream.

But the defibrillator was inside me now and there wasn't a damn thing I could do about it.

I was back on the gurney. I felt the brake release, and they wheeled me out of the operating room and to the elevator. The guy wearing khaki pants and a sports coat led the way. I finally remembered where I'd seen him before. He was the guy on the charter fishing boat, the *Sea Lover III*, the one who had followed Joe down to get some coffee.

Chapter Twelve

I didn't do much for the next week or so. The stitches under my left collarbone were healing nicely. A doctor came in one day and said so. I was confined to my room and I slept a lot and ate when they brought me food. It was starting to get to me, the solitude and the sensory deprivation. I needed something to do.

A personal trainer named Wade had started working with me on a stationary bike and some light dumbbells for about an hour every day, so at least I had that. It was something to look forward to. Wade was blond and muscular and spoke with a European accent. He looked and sounded like a personal trainer, like one in a movie or something. Nobody came to my room with an armed escort anymore. There was no need for it now that I had the defibrillator. All Freeze had to do was push a button and I was toast.

There was a bulge at the surgery site under my left collarbone and I could feel the device under my skin. It didn't make any noise or anything, but I could feel it with my fingers and I could feel its weight against my pectoral muscle. I was always aware of its presence. It was about the size and shape of a pocket watch.

They'd pinned a calendar to the wall by the bathroom door so I could keep track of the days leading up to the game.

The game was to start Wednesday, October 26.

On Saturday, October 22, a man came to my room and introduced himself as Frederick. He had a mustache and curly black hair and a gold hoop in his left ear. Bushy eyebrows. He wore an Adidas warm-up suit and running shoes. He pulled a tape measure out of his pocket and used it to measure the circumference of my neck.

"Are you going to make me a suit?" I said. "I've always wanted a tailored suit."

He laughed. "Not quite."

He handed me a small package, a cardboard box the size of a paperback novel with *G-29* printed on it in bold black lettering.

"What is it?" I said.

"Open it."

I opened the box and pulled out a suede pouch. I loosened the drawstring on the pouch and extracted the device, the G-29. It resembled one of those Bluetooth headsets people use with their cell phones. You hang it on your ear and it looks like you're walking around talking to yourself. Like some kind of mental patient. When I was a kid we had one phone in the house, a black rotary-dial made in the USA by Western Electric and leased by Ma Bell. It was indestructible. Wherever it is now, I would lay odds it still works. When you wanted to talk to someone, you dialed their number and they either answered or they didn't. If they didn't, you tried again later or forgot about it. You weren't tethered to the world twenty-four hours a day, seven days a week. It was a saner way to live.

I held the stupid little headset in the palm of my hand. "What's it for?" I said.

"We'll need to communicate with you from time to time during the game. It works like a walkie-talkie, but it receives and transmits on a dedicated frequency. Nobody except the party on the other end—Freeze or myself or an assigned proctor—will hear what you hear or what you say. All the players have one. We want you to start wearing it today to get used to it."

"And if I don't start wearing it today you're going to push a button on a remote control somewhere and fry my heart."

"I won't, personally, but Freeze might. Yes, that's pretty much the deal."

I wanted to ask him some questions. I wanted to know how Freeze got him and all the other guys to do the work they did for him. Did he pay them exorbitant sums of money? Were they coerced? Brainwashed? They all seemed pretty much normal, except for where they were and what they were doing. I wanted to ask him some questions, but I knew he wouldn't answer. Whatever we said would be heard over the intercom in my room, so even if Frederick *wanted* to talk to me I knew he would not.

I hung the thing on my ear, feeling depressed about it already.

"There," I said. "Happy?"

"I'm going to leave the room and go downstairs. In a few minutes, I'll try to contact you through the G-twenty-nine."

"OK," I said. "I'll wait here."

As if I had a choice.

I sat on the sofa. Several minutes passed and I didn't hear anything. I was starting to get worried. If Frederick was trying to talk to me and I wasn't answering, he might think I was intentionally ignoring him. He might tell Freeze, and then Freeze might decide to punch my ticket. I wasn't afraid to die, but I was afraid of what might happen to Juliet and Brittney if I didn't cooperate. Or even if I was *perceived* as not cooperating. I was starting to get worried, and then something struck me. Freeze wasn't going to kill me. At least not for some minor infraction like refusing to answer Frederick. I was an integral part of his demented little game. Without me, Snuff Tag 9 couldn't go on as scheduled. Freeze wasn't going to kill me. He needed me.

"Hello, Number Eight. Do you hear me?"

It was Frederick.

"Loud and clear," I said.

"Good. I want to check something. I want you to get up and walk around the room and listen for a series of beeps."

"I don't feel like it."

"Excuse me?"

"You didn't say Simon says."

"Number Eight, if you don't—"

"Tell Freeze I want to talk to him. Right now. He can call me on the intercom or he can call me on this piece of shit hanging on my ear. Either way will be fine. Tell him."

"Oh, I'll tell him all right. I'll tell him right away. In fact, I'll—"

"Just shut up and do it," I said.

I heard a click, and Frederick was gone. I sat there and twiddled my thumbs and whistled the theme song to the *Andy Griffith Show*. I sat there and waited and finally a voice came over the G-29.

But it was not the voice of Freeze, as I had requested.

It was the voice of my daughter, Brittney.

Chapter Thirteen

"Daddy?"

I couldn't believe it was her. The fact they had gotten to her so quickly gave me a sinking feeling in my gut.

"It's me," I said.

"Where are you?"

"I'm not sure. I'm not sure where I am, and if I knew I couldn't tell you. They're listening to everything I say."

"Oh my god, Dad. Everybody's looking for you. The FBI and everybody. What's going on? I was so worried. I haven't been able to sleep or eat or anything."

I started to respond, but I heard a click and the line went dead. Then another voice came on.

"Hello, Number Eight."

It was Freeze.

"Listen, motherfucker. If you touch a hair on her head—"

"Why were you rude to Frederick?" he said.

"Where is she? Where's my daughter?"

"Don't worry. She's at school, where she should be. We called her cell phone and patched her in to the G-twenty-nine. I just wanted you to know we have a bead on her should the need arise. All you have to do is make sure it doesn't. Again, why were you rude to Frederick?"

"I wanted to talk to you."

"You could have asked politely. Let me guess. You've gotten it into your head that I need you for the game, so you think you can behave any way you want. I've been doing this for a while, Number Eight. I've seen this kind of thing before, in varying degrees. I call it the Star Syndrome. You see it in the real world sometimes with upper-echelon musicians and professional ball players and other celebrities. They start believing their own hype, start thinking they're indispensable. Do you think you're indispensable? Let me assure you that you're not. One more display like the one with Frederick and you'll be watching your little girl get hurt. Real bad."

I clenched my fists and gritted my teeth and fought the urge to say what I wanted to say. *The only person who's going to get hurt real bad is you, you rotten motherfucker...*

I held my tongue. Maybe there was still hope. At least the FBI was looking for me. That was something. Maybe they had talked to Joe Crawford. I'd told Joe about the letter to Nathan Broadway, but I couldn't remember if I'd told him the location of the meeting place. I didn't think so. I'd been so sure the whole thing was a scam from a theft ring. So Joe wouldn't be able to tell the FBI much. They wouldn't have much to go on. Freeze had said that forty-five thousand people go missing every year in the United States alone. I guessed the FBI was looking for all of them. No, they were never going to find me. I was screwed and at the complete mercy of a madman. And at the moment, the only prudent thing to do was to tell him what he wanted to hear.

"I won't give you any more trouble," I said. "I apologize."

"There. That's better. Now what was it you wanted to talk to me about?"

"I would like to have some books and magazines and some movies. I'm bored out of my fucking mind in here. I'm going stir-crazy."

"It's all part of the regimen," he said. "No outside media. The game starts in four days. Believe me, you won't be bored then."

"I need something to pass the time. A crossword puzzle. Anything."

"Pass the time by planning your strategy to kill the eight other players. I don't know if you've wrapped your head around that yet or not, but that's what you're going to have to do. Kill. Eight. Other. People. It's the only way you yourself can possibly survive. If I were in your position, I would be riding that bike more and lifting the weights more. I would be praying and meditating, the way certain Native American tribesmen used to do before going into battle. I would be eating *all* of the food brought to me, not only half or three-quarters. I would—"

"All right. I see your point. I should be preparing myself for the game instead of whining about not having anything to do."

"Exactly. Now, are you ready to help Frederick calibrate the G-twenty-nine?"

"Sure. Whatever you say."

"Good. By the way, are you ever going to tell me about those scars on your hand?"

It was none of his business, but I figured what the hell. "I did some work in Tennessee a while back," I said. "A guy stomped my hand with the heel of his boot. Broke it all to shit. I've had six surgeries on it so far, but it's never going to work right again. As soon as it happened, I knew I wouldn't be able to play the guitar anymore."

"That must be tough. Does it hurt?"

"Constantly."

"That's good. Pain is good. A wounded animal is always more dangerous than a healthy one. Channel that pain into some fierceness, and maybe you won't be slaughtered the first day."

"Yeah. I might just surprise you."

"I hope so."

He disconnected. A few minutes later Frederick came back on and we did the tests on the G-29.

I exercised, and then dinner came. Filet mignon and a salad and a baked potato. I ate all of it, even the skin of the potato, which I usually throw away. Freeze was right. I hated to admit it, but he was right. I needed to gather as much strength as I could before the game started. All of the other players were younger than me, and they all had some kind of athletic talent. Soccer, basketball, tae kwon do. They were all college graduates, and I could tell by their photographs that they were all under the age of forty. The only thing I had on them, the only possible edge, was experience. I had faced death before, and I had killed before. Maybe the experience counted for something, but I wasn't sure how much. And the ex-military guys might have had some experiences of their own that matched or even exceeded mine. They might have seen combat, especially the SEAL. I figured he was probably the most dangerous of the bunch, the one to take out first if possible. I didn't have anything against any of these guys, but we'd all been dealt a nasty hand. If it came down to me or them, it was going to be them. I was sure they all felt the same way. It wasn't like any of us had much of a choice.

I took the chair from the desk and sat by the window for a while. It was dark outside, and there was some kind of frog clinging to the upper pane. His toes had suction cups on them. The light from the window attracted flying insects, and when one of them came within range the frog would open its mouth and lurch forward and in one swift motion devour its prey. It seemed like a clever ploy, but I wondered what that particular species did for meals millions of years ago before interior lighting and glass windows.

I watched the frog for over an hour, and then a second one showed up and, after that, a third. There didn't seem to be any competition over the food. There was plenty for everyone.

I shaved and took a shower and brushed my teeth. When I went back to the window the frogs were gone so I turned the light off and went to bed.

Chapter Fourteen

Tuesday night, the night before the game started, Frederick returned with another gadget. It was a plastic collar with cameras on it, like the one I'd seen in the video. It had a hinge on one side and a locking connector on the other. It was black and there were four lenses, front and back and left and right.

"Have a seat," Frederick said.

I sat on the desk chair and he gently wrapped the collar around my neck. I heard the plastic parts lock together with a click. It fit perfectly. Snugly enough that it wasn't going to move around a lot when I walked or ran, but not tight enough to choke me. The inside, the part next to my skin, was covered with soft fabric to prevent blisters.

"This is why you measured my neck the other night," I said.

"Yes."

"Seems like it might not be real comfortable to sleep in. How do I take it off?"

"You don't," he said. "And if you try, an alarm will go off in the central monitoring room. No, you'll be wearing the collar for the duration. I'm sure you'll get used to it."

"Do the cameras broadcast live during the game?"

"They do. Video only, but there are enough ambient microphones placed throughout the playing area to pick up audio from virtually any location. The cam-collars come on automatically, based on lighting conditions. They use the three-G network, same as cell phones, and they all run simultaneously. Nine players, four cameras each, so that's thirty-six live video feeds going to thirty-six LCD monitors. Plus, there are forty stationary cameras mounted at strategic locations around the field of play. Those go to forty more monitors, so seventy-six cameras and seventy-six monitors in all. We're able to capture all the action all the time. It's really quite remarkable."

"And all this is for Freeze's amusement?" I said.

"You know, boys and their toys."

"So do these collars run on batteries or what?"

"Yes," he said. "That's what I need to show you next."

He left the room for a minute and returned with a backpack and a shopping bag. The backpack was black and had a big white 8 painted on it. He unzipped it and showed me an inside compartment containing a rectangular steel box the size of a deck of cards. Another pocket contained a set of cables.

"This is the battery?" I said, pointing toward the steel box.

"This is the external battery pack. The internal battery in your unit lasts a long time, but if it ever starts running low, this is your backup. This cable is used to charge the internal battery while you sleep, and this one charges the external battery should the need arise." He pulled out a third cable. "And this one charges your G-twenty-nine. Like I said, the cameras are light-activated, which helps conserve power. There are nine little houses on the field—they're nothing more than garden sheds, really, with an army cot and a water spigot—and inside every house is a power outlet. Every player is assigned to a house."

"What's going to stop one of the other players from coming into my house and bashing my skull in with a rock while I sleep?"

"The game usually commences at sunrise and then stops at sunset. I thought Freeze would have told you all this by now."

"He didn't."

Frederick pulled a pamphlet out of the backpack. "Here's the complete set of rules, along with bios on all the players. You'll need to study this tonight. Anyone who deviates from the rules is punished immediately. The severity of the punishment depends on the severity of the infringement; but, needless to say, termination is always a possibility. Termination, that is, *death*, is always a possibility, as is watching someone you care about suffer."

"What's in the bag?"

"This is your uniform," he said.

He opened the shopping bag and pulled out a pair of black fatigue pants, a pair of black combat boots, and a red football jersey with the number 8 printed on the chest. There were three pairs of boxer briefs, three pairs of heavy cotton socks, and three undershirts.

"No jacket?" I said. "It's likely to get chilly out there in the swamp, especially early in the morning and at night."

I was half joking. I didn't figure Freeze gave a damn about our comfort, but Frederick responded with, "There will be a sleeping bag in your house, a down-filled mummy bag, so you'll be warm enough at night. And you will have the opportunity to obtain a jacket, but it's one of the things you'll have to earn along the way."

"What other things will we have the opportunity to earn?"

"Well, I don't want to tell you everything tonight. We like to keep some things a surprise. Makes it more interesting, don't you think?"

"Sure."

"You'll need to get a good night's sleep tonight, Number Eight. Tomorrow is going to be a long day. Let's hope it's long, anyway. If you don't watch yourself, it could be a very short day."

"I only get one shirt and one pair of pants?" I said, looking at the pile of clothes on the bed.

"Yes, so you need to take care of them best you can. They'll have to last the whole five days, if you make it to the finale. And if you don't, they'll be the clothes you're buried in. Farewell, Number Eight, and best of luck."

"Thanks," I said.

Chapter Fifteen

Frederick left the room and I tried on the uniform. Everything fit, even the boots.

Freeze had previously mentioned the possibility of obtaining weapons. I was wondering about that when another man came to my room, a man I hadn't met before. He wheeled in a metal cabinet with drawers labeled one to ten.

"I'm Zachary," he said. "It's time to choose your weapons."

Zachary was tall and thin. He wore a long white lab coat, a blue dress shirt with a button-down collar, and gray pants. Curly salt-and-pepper hair and a mustache. His eyes were red and he blinked all the time, like someone had just thrown sand in his face. I guessed it was a nervous condition.

I pointed toward the metal cabinet. "Got a machine gun in there somewhere?" I said.

"I'm afraid not. But each drawer contains a different weapon, and you're allowed to choose two. You tell me the numbers, and I open the drawers and hand you the weapons. What you end up getting is a matter of luck."

I knew all that from reading about the video game.

"Have all the other players chosen already?" I said.

"Yes, but every time an item is taken out of a drawer an identical one is put back in its place. That way everyone has a fair chance at getting one of the better items."

"Just out of curiosity, what ten weapons are in the drawers?" I said. I couldn't remember all of them from the Wikipedia article, and I wondered if they would even be the same.

"That's irrelevant. You'll get what you get."

"Like I said, just curious."

He started blinking like crazy. He seemed very nervous. He hesitated and then started counting the weapons off on his fingers. "There's a survival knife, a slingshot, a set of brass knuckles, a bullwhip, a pair of nunchucks, a policeman's nightstick, a two-foot length of tow chain, a fifty-caliber blowgun with three darts, a can of pepper spray, and a rechargeable eight-hundred-thousand-volt stun baton."

I stood there for a minute, trying to think about what I would pick if I had my choice. The slingshot or the blowgun would be good, because you could hurt someone from a distance. You could hurt them and then move in for the kill. All the other weapons would have to be used at close range. Depending on what you had at your disposal, close range could be risky as hell. If the other guy had a stun baton, for example, and all you had were some brass knuckles, your ass would be grass.

"Again, just out of curiosity, can you tell me what the other players got?" I said. I was trying to get a feel for what I would be up against.

"Absolutely not. That's part of the challenge, learning what weapons the other players have and then figuring out ways to defeat them."

"When I defeat someone, do I get to keep his weapons?"

"You obviously haven't read the rule book yet. No. When a player dies, his weapons die with him. You'll only have what you choose today."

"That sucks. I'd like to make an appeal for that rule to be changed."

More blinking. He knew I was fucking with him, but he couldn't help himself. "I need you to go ahead and choose now, Number Eight," he said, weariness in his voice and exasperation on his face.

When I was a kid, there was a show on television called *Let's Make a Deal*. The host was a guy named Monty Hall, and he would choose people from the studio audience to be contestants on the show. The people in the audience came dressed in outrageous costumes, hoping to get his attention and become contestants and win fabulous prizes. Monty Hall would walk up to a guy dressed like a rabbit or whatever and talk to him for a couple of minutes and then ask him to choose door number one, door number two, or door number three. One of the doors always had a great prize behind it, a washing machine or a recliner or a stove or some other big-ticket household item, and another would have something small but useful like a case of instant oatmeal. If you weren't lucky enough to choose either of those doors, you got the worthless booby prize behind the other one. Then there was the dealing part. Let's say the guy in the rabbit suit chose door number two, and let's say he got the good prize. Let's say he won a new television. Monty Hall would try to make a deal with him and get him to trade for what was behind a curtain on the other side of the stage. Sometimes there was a brand-new car behind the curtain, but most of the time it was a twelve-foot-high rocking horse or some other useless piece of crap. So it was a gamble. Rabbit Man had two choices. He could sit down and be happy with his new TV or he could go for the curtain and hope for the super duper mega prize. Of course the producers of that show knew greed was part of human nature. They knew most people would try to trade up for the better prize and therefore go home with nothing. But occasionally, just often enough to keep viewers tuned in, the guy in the rabbit suit would win the new car.

When I was a kid watching that show, I always wished I was psychic or had X-ray vision or something. If I had been psychic, or if I had had X-ray vision, I could have gone on the show and I could have taken Monty Hall for all he was worth. That was my wish, and that was around the time I came up with Rule #18 in Nicholas Colt's *Philosophy of Life*: Wish in one hand and spit in the other, and see which fills up first.

"I'll take drawer number four," I said.

He opened the drawer. It was the survival knife. He pulled it out and handed it to me. It had a black handle and a black leather sheath, and the blade was about seven inches long. It was a nice knife. I figured it would come in handy for all kinds of things, killing people being only one of them. I was happy with the choice I'd made. I felt I'd gotten lucky.

"One more," Zachary said.

"Seven."

"Are you sure you want drawer number seven?"

"Why, what's wrong with seven?"

"Nothing's wrong with it. Are you sure that's the one you want?"

He was trying to pull a Monty Hall on me, trying to put doubt in my mind. The most powerful weapon in the cabinet was the stun baton, and the least powerful the pepper spray. I figured drawer number seven contained one of the two. Zachary was trying to get me to give up the best weapon of the bunch, or he was trying to sway me from the booby prize.

I stood my ground. There was no point in second-guessing a decision wholly dependent on random chance. "I'm sure," I said. "Drawer number seven."

He opened it.

It wasn't the pepper spray, and it wasn't the stun baton. It wasn't the slingshot or the brass knuckles or the bullwhip. It wasn't the billy club, and it wasn't the tow chain or the fifty-caliber blowgun with three darts.

It was the nunchucks.

He handed them to me, two steel handles connected by a steel chain. Before I saw the collapsing rods inside, I thought the handles were only about four inches long. But with a flick of the wrist, they telescoped to three times that.

"You know how to use those?" Zachary said.

"Sure," I said. "I watched more than my share of martial arts flicks when I was a kid."

It was true. When I was thirteen, karate and everything that went along with it was all the rage. There were Bruce Lee movies at all the drive-in theaters, where you focused on the remarkable skill of the master and tried to ignore the terrible English over-dubs. There was a wandering Buddhist monk named Kwai Chang Caine on television, pretending to be a philosopher and a pacifist but kicking umpteen kinds of ass every week, and there was even a dopey little novelty song called "Kung Fu Fighting" playing on AM radio a thousand times a day.

I never had any money to buy real ones back then, so I made my own set of nunchucks. I cut about twelve inches off the wooden handles of a couple of garden tools, drilled holes in one end, and connected them with a strand of rawhide. I practiced whizzing them over my shoulder and between my legs like they did in the movies, often conking myself on the head or racking myself in the balls. Eventually I got pretty good with them, but when my stepfather found out I'd sawed the handles off the rakes he never used anyway, he took my nunchucks away and punched me in the jaw with his fist. That was about two years before he blew his own brains out with a .44 magnum.

Zachary shut the drawers and locked the cabinet. "Good-bye," he said. "And good luck."

The nunchucks were pretty cool, but I didn't know how effective they would be against some of the other weapons. I wanted the eight-hundred-thousand-volt stun baton.

"I'd like to trade for what's behind the curtain," I said.

Zachary turned and gave me a puzzled look and then pushed his cart out and disappeared.

I exercised for a while and practiced with the nunchucks. I did OK. I didn't conk myself in the head or rack my balls. I read the rule book twice and refamiliarized myself with the bios on the other players and went to bed at ten o'clock.

I was tired, but I couldn't sleep. One of the more interesting things in the rule book was the section on alliances. I was allowed to form a partnership with one other player, knowing eventually I would have to kill him or be killed by him. I didn't see how it would work, how you could trust someone who at any time might slit your throat or bash your head in, or zap you into submission with electrical current and then slit your throat or bash your head in. I figured I would go about Snuff Tag 9 the way I'd gone about most things in my life. I figured I would go it alone.

chapter Sixteen

I finally dozed off around four a.m. At five all the lights came on. An alarm sounded over the intercom, followed by the voice of Freeze.

"Good morning, gentlemen, and welcome to day one of Snuff Tag Nine. Please rise now and don your uniforms. Your escorts will be with you shortly. Best of luck to you all."

I shaved and brushed my teeth and put on the black fatigue pants and the boots and the red number 8 jersey. I crammed the disposable razor and the can of shaving cream and the toothbrush and tube of toothpaste and the soap and shampoo and deodorant and the spool of dental floss into my backpack. If possible, I wanted to bathe and shave every day. They say it helps keep your spirits up. That's what they tell potential prisoners of war. As an afterthought, I threw the notepad and pen from the desk in with the toiletries. Maybe I would chronicle this little adventure. Today seemed like a good day to get started on that memoir I'd always intended to write.

I amused myself with the absurdity of that thought for a second, and then I threaded my belt through the slots on the knife sheath, slid the blade in, and snapped the leather strap around the handle. I pushed the telescoping rods into the handles of the nunchucks and stowed them in the flap pocket on my right pants leg. I looked in the mirror. With the G-29 transceiver attached to my ear and the cam-collar wrapped around my neck, I looked like some sort of futuristic rugby player.

My eyes were bloodshot from sleep deprivation, but otherwise I looked OK. I was well nourished and well hydrated and physically fit, and my clarity of thought seemed as though it had actually improved over the past couple of weeks. Maybe it was because I hadn't had any alcohol. In my normal routine there are days I don't drink, but there aren't that many of them. Alcohol wasn't an addiction for me, like cigarettes had been and, more recently, narcotics, but it was a habit I was starting to think I might do well to give up. Then again, I probably wasn't going to live through the day, so it didn't make much sense to start worrying about lifestyle changes now. Like it or not, I was on the wagon, and I would probably never get the opportunity to fall off.

A few minutes after I got dressed, Wade came in and handed me a black bandana. Wade was my personal trainer. I hadn't seen him in a few days. He wore a navy-blue warm-up suit and too much cologne. His short blond hair was still wet from the shower.

"How do you feel?" he said.

"Not bad, considering I only got one hour of sleep."

"Don't worry. All the players are anxious. Some of them didn't get any."

"You want me to put this on now?" I said. I knew what the bandana was for. The rule book said all of us would be blindfolded until we got to the playing field. I guessed Freeze didn't want anyone to know the exact location of the game, even though only one man would walk out of the swamp alive.

"Yes," Wade said. "It's time."

I wrapped the cloth around my head and tied it in the back. Wade checked it out to make sure I hadn't left any peepholes.

"Does someone usually get killed the first day?" I said.

"Someone *always* gets killed the first day. Freeze makes sure of it. I want you to walk behind me, with your right hand on my right shoulder. We'll take the elevator to the first floor and from there I'll lead you to the bus."

"Bus?" I said. It didn't make sense to let all the players ride together. What was going to stop one of them from taking his bandana off and going on a quick little killing spree?

Wade must have read my mind.

"Nobody's allowed to make a move during the transport," he said. "If they do, they'll be terminated immediately."

"I keep forgetting everybody has one of these defibrillator things wired to their heart. I guess it's good in a way. Everyone has to follow the rules or risk getting zapped."

"It's extreme, but effective," Wade said. "You ready?"

"Ready as I'll ever be."

I put my hand on his shoulder and followed him out of the room that had been my home for the past two weeks. It had been a safe and comfortable abode, and I knew with certainty that the place I was headed to was going to be neither.

Chapter Seventeen

Wade sat next to me on the bus. We rode in silence for a while, and then he quizzed me on some of the rules.

"When does the game begin each day?"

"When the alarm sounds once," I said. "Usually around sunrise."

"And when does it end?"

"When the alarm sounds twice. Sunset."

"Are any sorts of engagements allowed at night, between sunset and sunrise?"

"No."

"That's right. Unless Freeze says so. When are you allowed to use your weapons?"

"When the alarm sounds three times. Otherwise, weapons are illegal."

"Yes. And when the alarm sounds four times, it means the weapons period is over. What happens if you're caught using a weapon during a period when they've been prohibited?"

"Immediate termination," I said. "No warning."

The player in the seat behind me started crying. I could hear his sobs. I wondered which one it was. I knew it wasn't Number

Seven, the former Navy SEAL who was a diving instructor in Florida now, and I knew it wasn't Number Six, the pilot who got his training in the Marine Corps. I was pretty sure those guys had faced death before. Maybe many times. Maybe it was Number One, the insurance salesman from Waterloo with a black belt in tae kwon do. Or Number Two, the computer programmer who played tennis at Stanford. Whoever it was, I started thinking of him as a weakling. I started thinking I would rip his whiny little face off with my bare hands as soon as I got half a chance. Freeze had gotten to me already, had stripped away part of my humanity. It was kill or be killed, and today was day one. There was no time to feel sorry for anyone, no time to think about anything but survival. I didn't want to murder any of these guys, but I had no choice. It was them or me, and I had no intention of allowing it to be me.

"Shut the fuck up," I said to the crier.

Wade grabbed my arm, whispered in my ear. "Relax, Number Eight. I've been around since the first season of Snuff Tag Nine, and I've seen this kind of thing more than once. Sometimes the guy really is crying, and other times he's putting on a show to make the others *think* he's weak."

Wade was right. I felt like an idiot. I'd almost forgotten Rule #11 in Nicholas Colt's *Philosophy of Life*: Never underestimate your opponent. Maybe the guy was a genuine pansy or maybe he was the best hustler on the planet.

On my thirty-first birthday I went to a nightclub in Jacksonville called Harlow's. I went there with Joe Crawford. Joe and I were both single at the time, no wives, no girlfriends, and we were out for a night of heavy drinking and blues music. We'd taken a cab downtown and planned to take a cab home. Matt Murphy was scheduled to play, and his band included a bass player named Donald Dunn who'd done some studio work with me a few years previously. I was sipping my drink and talking to

Joe, waiting for the band to come on, thinking I would chat with
Donald and Matt after their first set, when a short, dark-haired
guy wearing a navy-blue nylon jacket grabbed me by the arm and
said, "Jacksonville Sheriff's Office. We need you to step outside."

Another guy in another navy-blue nylon jacket was already
pushing Joe toward the door. I'd had a few drinks and I knew I
hadn't done anything wrong and I sort of copped an attitude with
the asshole who had me in a wristlock.

"I want to see your badge," I said.

"Here's my badge, motherfucker."

He opened the nylon jacket. The badge was mounted on his
belt. It looked real, and so did the semiautomatic pistol holstered
beside it.

"What's this all about?" I said.

"Just step outside."

We stepped outside, and there were four police cruisers
parked near the door with their red and blue lights flashing. The
officer who'd escorted me out, whose name I later learned was
Esselsyn, took my driver's license and Joe's driver's license and
read the numbers into his walkie-talkie. A few minutes later he
told us what was going on.

"We got a call from one of the bartenders," he said. "Thought
the two of you looked like a pair named Hodges and Kelper. You
heard about them?"

"I heard about them," I said. "They're wanted for murder.
They drive along and randomly blast other cars with a shotgun.
You thought we were them?"

"Bartender called the hotline with the tip, we had to check it
out."

"So we're free to go?" I said.

"Yeah."

And that was it. Officer Esselsyn didn't apologize for roust-
ing us out of the bar, didn't offer to buy us a drink or anything.

When we went back inside, the bartender who had made the call showed us some pictures of Hodges and Kelper that had been published in that morning's edition of the *Florida Times-Union*.

Right away I saw why the bartender had made the mistake. The resemblance was uncanny. Hodges and Kelper looked like genetically inferior versions of Joe and me. They looked like the ugly versions. Our evil twins. It made me think about how being in the wrong place at the wrong time and looking like someone else can screw your life up forever. Innocent people go to prison. Innocent people get executed. It happens. It probably happens more often than anyone wants to admit.

The ordeal had my heart pounding, much as it was pounding now. I was on my way to the swamp with a busload of guys who wanted to kill me. Random chance had put me here. Wrong place, wrong time. If one of the two private investigators ahead of me in the phone book had answered Nathan Broadway's call, I wouldn't be dealing with this shit right now. I would have never heard of Freeze and The Sexy Bastards and Snuff Tag 9. It was all so ridiculous and absurd, just like the night Joe and I got hustled out of Harlow's by JSO homicide detectives for crimes we didn't commit.

"You OK?" Wade said.

"Yeah. I was just thinking about something."

"Want to talk about it?"

"I don't belong here," I said. "This was never supposed to be me. It's like the time I was almost locked up for someone else's crime. It's just—"

"You going to start crying, like that guy back there?"

"Fuck you, Wade. You're not the one on the way to the slaughterhouse."

"You don't have to die," he said. "You just have to win the game."

"Do you think I even have a shot?"

He hesitated. "It doesn't matter what I think. All that matters is what *you* think. You have to believe in yourself. You have to, or you'll never make it through day one."

I took a deep breath. I sensed we were getting close to our destination.

"All right," I said. "Let's go over the rules again."

And we did.

Chapter Eighteen

The bus slowed and made a series of turns and then hissed to a stop.

"Are we there yet?" I said.

"We're there," Wade said. "I want you to put your hand on my shoulder, same as you did when we left your room. I'm going to lead you to your house, where you'll be staying for the duration of the game."

"OK."

We disembarked, and I kept my hand on Wade's shoulder. We started out on pavement, moved to what felt like a trail lined with pine needles, and finally walked into some fairly heavy underbrush. We trudged through the thickets and thistles at a lazy pace for maybe thirty minutes. I figured we traveled a mile or so west of the beaten path. I knew it was west because the sun was directly behind us. I heard a splash at one point, a small one like a fish jumping, and Wade told me we were walking past a pond. A few minutes later we stopped.

"You can take your blindfold off now," Wade said.

I took my blindfold off. We were standing in a clearing, and at the center of the clearing was a wood-frame structure the size of a large garden shed. It had cedar lap siding and a window and a metal roof. It was yellow with white trim. It looked like a kid's playhouse. There was even a small front porch with a brass number 8 tacked to one of the support posts.

"Home sweet home," I said. "Can I go inside?"

"Absolutely. This is your place. You can do anything you want to here. Within the constraints of the game, of course."

I stepped onto the wooden porch and opened the door and walked inside. Wade followed me in. There was a cot against one wall with white sheets and a pillow and a sleeping bag rolled up at the foot. A plywood cabinet concealed the plumbing to a stainless steel sink and chrome faucet mounted against the opposite wall.

"Where's the bathroom?" I said.

Wade laughed. "I'm afraid you're on your own, Number Eight. There's a roll of toilet paper under the sink."

"What about food?"

"The swamp is your smorgasbord. All you can eat. Free."

"You're joking, right? Can't I get a pizza delivered up here or something?"

"Consider yourself lucky. This is the first year we've piped running water into the houses. Too many players were falling out from dehydration, so Freeze spent about a hundred grand on some deep wells and basic plumbing. Beats the hell out of boiling swamp water to drink."

I was still concerned about the food situation. "I have a knife and a pair of nunchucks," I said. "What am I going to do, sneak up on a squirrel and slit its throat?"

"Surviving out here is all part of the game. If you live long enough to get hungry, you'll find a way."

"Thanks for trying to cheer me up," I said.

Wade took a step toward the door. "Time for me to go now, Number Eight. Best of luck to you."

"Thanks."

We shook hands. I stood on the porch and watched him cross the clearing and disappear into the woods.

I looked at my watch. It was 9:37. I went back into the house and got a drink of water and opened the door to the cabinet under the sink. There was a roll of toilet paper in there, as Wade had promised, and a towel and a washcloth and a bar of Ivory soap. There was also a steel frying pan, which seemed useless at the moment. Even if I was able to kill a bird or a rabbit or something, it was going to be next to impossible to start a fire. I wasn't a Boy Scout. I didn't know how to strike up a flame by rubbing two sticks together. Freeze could have spent an extra buck and provided us with a box of matches or a butane lighter, but he didn't. He wanted to see who could survive five days in the swamp with barebones supplies and eight opposing players out for blood. Old Freeze. Old sport. What a game he had devised. If I made it out of this alive, I planned to spend every waking moment for the rest of my life thinking of a way to kill the fat son of a bitch.

I tossed my backpack on the floor, reclined on the cot, and stared at the ceiling and waited. There was nothing else to do. Soon I would be forced to kill someone for no good reason. I would be forced to kill someone for the fat man's amusement. I was exhausted. I had only slept an hour. I closed my eyes for a minute, knowing I shouldn't, and fell into a restless sleep poisoned with bizarre dreams. I was climbing some sort of jungle gym, and I kept climbing and climbing, trying to reach the top, but when I looked upward the steel bars went on to infinity, and when I looked downward they descended into a bottomless pit. I climbed higher and higher, my lungs burning and my muscles screaming in pain, and suddenly I was in a white room with black curtains and my father was there talking to me. This was my biological father, not my stepfather. My stepfather committed suicide when I was fifteen. My biological father was still alive, as far as I knew. I'd only met him once, when I was twenty-five. We got drunk on wine at an Italian restaurant and then he bought me dinner. A salad and a plate of spaghetti. It was the only time he ever bought me anything. I had only met him once, and now he was in this white room with black curtains talking to me in my dream.

"Pretend they're me," he said.

"What do you mean?" I said. "I don't understand."

"Pretend the men in the game are me. Then it will be easier to kill them. That's what you want, isn't it? You want to kill me. Pretend they're me, and it will be easier."

"I don't want to kill anybody."

"Yes, you do, Nicholas. Yes, you do. You want to kill me. You've always wanted to."

"Seriously. I just want another glass of wine. And some more spaghetti."

We sat at a white table in the white room and passed a silver cup back and forth. We passed it back and forth and I lit a cigarette and the smoke curled between my lips and nostrils and I inhaled it deeply and felt a euphoric calm wash over me.

"Are you still hungry?" my father said.

"No. Not anymore."

"Kill me, then. Do it now, and then we can eat."

I laughed, knowing what he said didn't make any sense. I laughed and I took another drag on the cigarette, and an obnoxious high-pitched piercing wail penetrated my eardrums and drilled its way into the core of my brain.

It was the alarm. Time to play the game.

Chapter Nineteen

I sprang out of bed and pulled my knife from its sheath, and then I remembered you couldn't use weapons unless the alarm sounded four times. It had only sounded once. At least that's what I thought. I put the knife back and secured it and looked out the window. Nothing.

The audio on the G-29 earpiece buzzed to life and a voice said, "Hello, Number Eight."

"Hello," I said. "Who's this?"

"You can call me Ray. There are two boxes under your cot. I want you to pull out the one on your left."

"OK."

I knelt down and looked under the cot. There were two boxes. I hadn't noticed them before. The one on the right was the size of a shoebox. The one on the left was much smaller, like a box for a wristwatch or a necklace. I grabbed the smaller box on the left, as Ray had instructed.

"Do you have the box?" he said.

"Yes."

"Open it."

I opened it. It was a compass. An old-fashioned compass the size of a stopwatch, with a brass housing and a glass face.

"It's a compass," I said.

"I want you to leave your house and start walking north," Ray said.

I had wondered how they were going to orchestrate the battles, and now I knew. Each player was given a compass and instructed to travel in a certain direction. Eventually the players Freeze wanted to match up would collide. I took the toiletries out of the backpack and stowed them under the sink with the toilet paper and the washcloth and the bar of Ivory soap and tossed the notepad and pen on the cot under my pillow. I walked out to the porch and looked at the compass and headed north. It was ten fifteen. The sky was clear, and the sun to my right beamed dots of brightness through the canopy. Cameras everywhere, mounted on poles and tree branches. They didn't try to hide them. No sound but the occasional chirp from a bird or rustle from a squirrel or electric servo from a camera tracking me as I made my way through the brush. I walked by an area roped off with the red plastic tape they used to define boundaries. I was tempted to duck under the tape and sprint eastward. To the east was the road the bus had come in on. To the east was freedom. But I remembered the video and knew better than to veer to the other side of the tape. Doing so would mean instant death. I had no choice but to continue north, the direction Ray had dictated.

I walked into a clearing and Ray said, "Stop. Be on your guard, Number Eight. Your first opponent will arrive soon."

I stopped, looked in every direction, didn't see anyone. I backed up against an oak tree and waited. Listened. There was a fat branch low enough for me to reach, so I heaved myself up and climbed high enough to be hidden by the leaves. Ray didn't say anything, so I must not have broken any rules. There was a camera mounted to a branch a few feet away from me. Its servo hummed to life and the lens swiveled in my direction. I felt like giving it the finger or sticking my tongue out at it or something, but I didn't. Freeze had me by the balls and there was no point in antagonizing him. As much as I wanted to, there was no point in it.

I was in a good spot. I was in the catbird seat. Literally. From my tree branch I could see the entire clearing, so no chance of my opponent sneaking up on me. I waited. Sweat trickled down my back, and blood swished through my arteries in bounding waves. I was hyperalert. The short nap had done me good.

I scanned the area left to right, and then in my peripheral vision I saw him. You could see those red jerseys they gave us from a mile away. It was Number Two, the computer programmer from Hannibal, Missouri. The Stanford graduate. The tennis player. It made sense that Freeze matched us up. He was six feet tall and weighed one sixty-five, about the same as me. About the same as me before I was abducted. I think I'd lost a few pounds since then. There was a slingshot sticking out of one of Number Two's pockets, and it looked like another pocket was full of ammunition, rocks or whatever. I couldn't see his second weapon. It would have been hard to conceal the bullwhip, the nightstick, the tow chain, the blowgun, or the stun baton, so I figured his other weapon was the brass knuckles or the pepper spray or the collapsible nunchucks. Or the survival knife. My knife was fairly well concealed under the tails of my jersey, so his could have been too. He crept along the perimeter of the clearing, eyes darting here and there at the least sound. He was nervous. More nervous than I was, if that was possible. He didn't want this any more than I did. But one of us had to die. That was the deal. In a matter of minutes, one of us wouldn't be breathing anymore.

I waited for him to stroll past the tree, thinking I would pounce from above and finish him with no warning. I would knock him to the ground with my momentum and then break his neck with a quick jerk. But he never strolled past the tree. He did something I never would have expected. He walked to the center of the clearing and sat on the ground. He folded his legs in the lotus position and just sat there with his eyes closed. It looked like he was meditating.

It was a clever thing to do, when I thought about it. From his position he could hear if anyone started to come his way, and he had time to get up and prepare himself for a response. It would have been a bad move if the weapons alarm had sounded. If the weapons alarm had sounded, another player with a slingshot or a blowgun or even a knife could have wounded him from a distance and then moved in for the kill. But the weapons alarm had not sounded. No weapons allowed. Breaking that rule meant instant termination, so nobody was going to break that rule. So Number Two was smart. Sitting at the center of the clearing was as good as or better than being hidden in the treetops. Better, I decided. If someone saw me and climbed up after me I had nowhere to go. This wasn't a Hollywood movie, and my name wasn't Tarzan. There were no vines to grab on to and swing to another tree. One of the stronger players could grab my leg and yank me down and that would probably be it. The fall would probably kill me. No more climbing up in trees, I decided, unless weapons were green-lighted. Then it would be a different ball game.

"Time to engage, Number Eight," Ray said.

"I'm still planning my strategy," I said.

"Time to engage. You have sixty seconds to climb down from that tree. Starting now."

I looked across the clearing at Number Two. His eyes were still closed. Good-looking kid. I was sure his parents were very proud of him. Second seed on the tennis team at Stanford. Good job now as a computer programmer. Good money, bright future. And today it would all come to a screeching halt. Today it would come to a brutal and violent end, because it was him or me, and it damn sure wasn't going to be me.

"Thirty seconds, Number Eight," Ray said.

"Fuck. All right, I'm coming down."

I climbed down from the tree and sprinted toward Number Two. His eyes opened wide and he stood and took a defensive position. Like a boxer. I guess he thought we were going to have a bare-knuckle fistfight, but that wasn't what I had in mind. I barreled toward him, and when I got close I dived in with my shoulder aimed at his knee. In football it would have been called a personal foul. In football my team would have been penalized fifteen yards. But this wasn't football. We were fighting for our lives. Everything was fair.

I tried to clip his knee with my shoulder, but he dodged the blow and I tumbled into a somersault and landed back on my feet. Before I had a chance to fully recover, to fully regain my balance, he came at me like a bullet and head-butted me in the gut. I stumbled backward and fell to the ground. He'd knocked the wind out of me. I couldn't breathe. He straddled me and started pummeling me in the face with his fists. He caught me with a couple of good ones to the nose, and I tasted the blood as it trickled down my throat. Now it was even harder to breathe. For a second the world went purple and I thought I was going to pass out. That would have been the end of me. But I didn't pass out. He hit me squarely in the jaw with his right hand, and I heard something crack. It wasn't my jaw. It was his hand. He'd broken his hand. My face was going to be bruised badly where he hit me, but he got the worst of it. His hand was shattered. I heard the bones crunch. It sounded like someone stepped on a box of pencils.

"Shit!" he shouted. He got up and cupped his right hand in his left and held it against his chest and paced around in tight circles. He was obviously in excruciating pain. You could see it in his face. His eyes and lips were screwed into an expression of extreme agony.

I managed to rise and stumble toward him. Dazed and dizzy. It felt like the earth beneath me was falling away. He swung with a left hook, but I ducked and nailed him with a solid punch to the rib cage. While he was still trying to figure out what hit him, I grabbed his busted hand and squeezed it as hard as I could. His ears turned purple and his eyes rolled back in his head. I kept squeezing until he fell to his knees. His pained expression turned to one of resignation. He was done. He knew it was all over for him. I cocked my right arm, intending to give him a karate chop to the windpipe and finish him off, but before I delivered the fatal blow the alarm wailed three times in quick succession. That meant weapons were allowed now. No point in risking an injury to my hand, I thought, so I went for the blade.

I was going to slit his throat, but a split second after I gripped the knife's handle a million volts of electric-blue acid flooded my eyeballs. It was the pepper spray. He'd reached into a pocket and pulled it out as soon as the alarm sounded. He'd pulled it out and sprayed it directly at my face. He'd beaten me to the draw. Now I was blind, and a mixture of tears and snot and saliva and blood flowed from my eyes and nose and mouth and dribbled off my chin like a leaky faucet. The tables had turned. He had the advantage now. I couldn't see a damn thing.

I pulled the knife from its sheath and started swiping wildly at the air, hoping to fend off any further assaults, hoping to keep him at bay until my vision cleared. I knew he couldn't operate the slingshot with one hand. No way. I was enjoying a measure of satisfaction in knowing that when he started pelting me in the head with the rocks from his pocket. He was throwing with his left hand, so the stones weren't traveling at the velocity they would have been with his right, but they were traveling fast enough. They hurt, and I felt cuts open up on the right side of my neck and my right cheek. Then one hit me dead center in the forehead. He must have heaved it with all his might, with all he had left. It hit me like a sledgehammer. My knees went weak. I was going down. I struggled to stay on my feet, but it was no use. I'd suffered too many blows to the head.

I fell to the ground. My vision had partially returned, but everything was green and distorted and blurred. Like looking through a Coke bottle. I held the knife up with both hands in a final gesture of defense, but he had me now. He had me, and we both knew it. He was going to live, and I was going to die.

He staggered toward me. The strength drained from my arms. They fell limp to my sides. I still had the knife, but I couldn't wrap my fingers tightly enough around the handle for it to be of any use. I was helpless. All he had to do was crush my skull with the heel of his boot. It's what I would have done. He positioned himself and lifted his leg to do just that. Like he'd read my mind.

And then a miracle happened.

Chapter Twenty

Number Two grabbed the side of his neck with his only hand that still worked. He grabbed the side of his neck and pulled something out and looked at it. While he stared at whatever it was he pulled out, another red jersey entered my warbled field of vision and the man wearing it grabbed Number Two by the hair and jerked his head back and opened his throat with a survival knife identical to mine. The gash was enormous. It nearly decapitated him. Number Two fell to the ground in a bloody heap.

I looked at the man standing over him, strained the number on his jersey into focus. It was Number Five. The architect from Bainbridge, Georgia. The marathon runner. He'd killed Number Two, and now he was coming for me.

"Wait," I said. "You don't have to do this."

He didn't say anything. He was nervous as a cat. He was circling around me and looking in all directions, making sure someone didn't surprise him like he'd surprised Number Two.

"Please," I said. "I know a way out of this."

He didn't stop moving. Kept circling. He glanced at me and snarled, "What the fuck you talking about?"

"I know a way to get these things out of our chests."

"Impossible," he said. "They're booby-trapped. If you try to take them out, they discharge into your heart and kill you."

"I know a way."

"What way?"

"You don't have to kill me. We can form an alliance. My trainer said we're allowed to do that. We can team up."

"Why would I want to form an alliance with you?"

"It might not look like it at the moment, but I'm a good fighter. And I've faced death before. I'm not going to freak out under pressure. And I can show you a way to get the defibrillator out of your chest once this thing is over."

"Only one of us can win the game. Even if we team up, one of us will have to die eventually. If I let you live now, you might kill me later. There's really no reason for me to take that chance."

"I might know a way out of that too. I might know a way we can both walk out of this alive. Think about what life is going to be like even if you win. You'll be relegated to a foreign country, and you'll still have that death machine wired into your chest. You'll still be under Freeze's control for the rest of your life. Let me live and I'll give you some names. Then, if you win, they'll help you remove the defibrillator and you'll be free. You can even come back and kick Freeze's ass if you want to."

"I know people too. I know some of the best architects and engineers on the planet. If they can't figure out how—"

"Do you know a surgeon who won the Nobel Prize?"

The alarm sounded twice, which indicated a time-out period. Nobody was allowed to attack until the alarm sounded one time again. Number Five stopped circling me. He took a deep breath.

"You're full of shit," he said. "You're just making things up as you go along, fabricating everything in a desperate attempt to save your own life. For one thing, Freeze and the boys are listening to everything we say over the G-twenty-nines. If you really did know about such a surgeon, you wouldn't be advertising it to them." He paused. I had the feeling he would have killed me then and there if the time-out alarm hadn't sounded. "Forming an alliance with a stranger goes against my better judgment, but you might be of some use to me. I might be able to use you to lure another player into a trap or something. Get up. Consider yourself a prisoner of war."

I thought about that. Maybe this was it for me. Maybe today was my day to catch the bus. Maybe it was in the cards. I didn't want to die, but I wasn't going to let him use me for bait. I was already Freeze's prisoner. I wasn't going to be Number Five's as well.

"Forget it," I said. "We can be equal partners, or nothing. You can kill me now, but I'm not going to be your bitch."

He looked me directly in the eyes. His expression was unchanging. I could see the pulse in his neck. "You got balls. I'll say that. Double-cross me and I'll cut them off and feed them to you."

"So we have a deal?"

"Whatever. Yeah. We have a deal."

He offered his hand. We locked wrists, and he helped me to a standing position.

"I must look like something from a horror movie," I said.

"Something like that. Come on. Let's go get you cleaned up."

"My place or yours?"

"Yours. You lead the way."

I opened the compass and started walking south, back toward my house. Number Five fell in behind me.

"For this to work," I said, "we're going to have to trust each other. You watch my back, I watch yours. If one of us gets in trouble, the other comes to the rescue."

"That seems to be the arrangement."

"In order to establish some of that trust, it might help to know some things about each other."

"What things?" he said. "You want me to tell you my life's story?"

"Just the good parts."

"You don't have a high enough security clearance for me to tell you anything about myself. In fact, you don't have any security clearance at all."

I wondered what he was talking about. Security clearance. He must have been employed by a government agency. Not part of the bio I'd seen.

"I already know a few things," I said. "I know you're an architect, and I know you're a serious long-distance runner. I know you're from Bainbridge."

"The only information you have on me is what Freeze gave you, and that's all the information you're going to get."

"Ever go to war?" I said.

"None of your business."

"Ever been married?"

"Again, none of—"

"OK, enough about you. Let's talk about me. I was born in Jeffersonville, Indiana, right across the river from Louisville, Kentucky. My father joined the navy while my mother was pregnant, and he ended up getting stationed at the naval air station in Jacksonville. He moved my mother and me there when I was still a baby. My mother and father divorced when I was two, and then my mother married a drunken asshole named Tyler Walker. All I remember is them shouting and cussing at each other every day until my mother died in a car wreck when I was five. My father was out of the picture, so I got stuck with Tyler. He took me fishing sometimes and taught me how to shoot a gun, but most of the time he stayed plastered. Anytime something went wrong he blamed me. He beat me with a belt or a strip of Hot Wheels track or whatever else was handy. One time I was washing his car and I accidentally broke the radio antenna, and he beat me with that.

I still have scars on the back of my legs from that beating. When I was twelve—"

"You're annoying me, Number Eight. I really don't care about any of that shit. All I want to do is make it through the next five days without getting my ass killed. I don't care about your lousy childhood, and I don't care about—"

"I was a rock star," I said.

"What?"

"In the eighties. Southern rock and blues. I had mansions on both coasts, flew to gigs in chartered jets. Booze, drugs, a different chick every night. The whole nine yards. I'm not allowed to tell you my name, but if I did you would recognize it. My songs still get airplay on the classic rock stations."

"That's cool, I guess. But it really doesn't have anything to do with our situation right now, does it? Being a former rock star isn't going to save your ass from the six other guys who want to kill you."

"Five."

"What?"

"Five other guys who want to kill me. There's me and you and five others left. You killed Number Two, remember?"

"Yeah, but there's going to be a ninth player. We don't know who it is or when they're coming, but there's going to be a ninth."

"Right. I almost forgot."

"My trainer told me some things about the ninth player," he said.

"Like what?"

"He said it's always a very dramatic scene when they bring in Number Nine. Freeze makes movies from this shit and shares them with his rich friends. You knew that, right?"

"Nobody ever told me, but I thought it might be something like that."

"Yeah. Reality TV for sadists. Anyway, my trainer said there's always this big drama when Number Nine is introduced. Usually

it's someone that one of the other players cares about. It's someone they care about dearly, like a brother or a cousin or a best
friend or something. Can you imagine?"

"What would you do?" I said. "What would you do if you
were forced to go against your brother?"

"What could I do? I would have to kill him. I wouldn't have
a choice."

I didn't say anything. We walked on. My eyes were still
stinging from the pepper spray, and my face felt like it had gone
through a meat grinder. After a few minutes I broke the silence.
I wanted Number Five to be on my side, and I thought sharing
some things from my past might help.

"Being a former rock star isn't going to save my ass from the
guys who want to kill me," I said, "but I've been through some shit
that might."

"What shit?"

"I was the sole survivor of a plane crash. Let me back up a
minute. I'd gotten tired of the coke and the smoke and the kinky
road bitches, and I decided to clean up my act a bit. Soon after I
did, we were doing a show in Kingston, Jamaica, and I met the
most beautiful woman on the planet. Her name was Susan. I took
her on the road with me and eventually we got married. Our picture as bride and groom was on the cover of Rolling Stone magazine. We didn't know it at the time, but Susan was pregnant with
our daughter, Harmony, when that picture was taken. Long story
short, I watched them and all the members of my band roast in
the wreckage of a chartered jet. For some reason I lived and they
died. And it's been that way all my life. Bad luck follows me, but
I always seem to walk away from it somehow. And I'll walk away
from this Snuff Tag Nine thing too. Stick with me and don't do
anything stupid and we might both get to walk away."

"I don't believe in luck," Number Five said. "If I walk away
from this, it will be because I'm a better man than the others.

Because I'm smarter and have a higher level of patience. Better endurance. It's the way I've won races, and it's the way I'll win this."

"What if it's me and you in the finale?" I said.

"Won't happen. I'll have to kill you before that. But if by some miracle it does happen, I'll take you in five seconds. No offense, but I wouldn't even break a sweat with you."

"No offense taken," I said. "But you should never underestimate your opponent. That's always a mistake."

"Is that your house up there?"

"Yeah. That's it. I'll get cleaned up, and then we can talk about how we're going to eliminate the other players."

When we were about thirty yards from my house, the alarm sounded once. The time-out period was over. The game was on again. On like Donkey Kong. It sounded once, followed by three staccato bursts. The game was on, and weapons were allowed.

In one swift motion I swiveled and pulled my knife from its sheath and buried it in Number Five's gut.

Chapter Twenty-One

He looked at me in astonishment. The assault had caught him totally by surprise. He hadn't expected it, and the truth was neither had I.

I twisted the blade and then yanked it out. A thread of bright red blood oozed from the corner of Number Five's mouth, and he fell to the ground. He never went for his knife. He never said another word or took another breath. He died silently at my feet.

It wasn't the first time I'd taken another man's life, but it was the first time I'd done so when there was no immediate threat to my own. I felt sick about it. There was an acid-soaked sewer rat writhing around in my gut, twisting and gnashing and trying to claw its way out. I felt sick about killing Number Five, but it was what I had to do. The alliance wasn't going to work. He was going to eliminate me as soon as it was no longer convenient to have me around. He'd practically said so. *I wouldn't even break a sweat with you*, he'd said. Big mistake. His hubris had gotten him killed.

The alarm sounded twice. Time-out again. I wondered why so soon, but I wasn't going to complain. The more time-outs the better. A perpetual time-out would have suited me just fine.

I wanted Number Five's blowgun and his darts, but taking weapons from a dead player was against the rules. I left him lying there and walked toward my house. I wanted to get cleaned up before the time-out period ended.

I was disturbed by what Number Five had said about the ninth player. Almost always someone one of the other players cared dearly about, he'd said. I was disturbed because now I knew who Number Nine was going to be. Number Nine was going to be Joe Crawford. My best friend since sixth grade. My best friend in the whole world.

The armed escort the day my defibrillator was implanted, the guy wearing khaki pants and a sports coat, had been on the *Sea Lover III* with us. The charter fishing boat. He had followed Joe to the lower deck to get some coffee. Joe had given him a business card. That's what that was all about. Now they knew Joe was my friend, and they knew where he lived. They were going to abduct him and surgically implant a defibrillator in him and force him to play the game. Joe was going to be Number Nine. I was almost sure of it. Thinking about it made my stomach churn even more. Joe was going to be Number Nine, and I was going to be dead. Number Five had said he would kill his own brother if it came down to it, but not me. Joe was the closest thing I ever had to a brother, and I would die for him without hesitation. I would sacrifice my own life to save his. No way I was going to kill him.

Which meant I was going to die.

I made it to the house and walked inside and turned the faucet on. I splashed water on my sore face and dabbed it dry with a towel. Assessed my wounds with my fingertips. The cuts from the rocks Number Two had thrown at me weren't deep. They weren't even really cuts. More like abrasions. They weren't deep, but they hurt. My jaw hurt too, especially when I clenched my teeth.

A voice came over the G-29. It was Ray again.

"Get the other box under your cot," he said. "Pull it out and open it."

I pulled it out and opened it. It was about the size of a shoe-box, and it was filled with first-aid supplies. I opened the bottle of hydrogen peroxide and dribbled some onto a square of gauze and dabbed my abrasions. I squeezed some triple antibiotic oint-ment onto them and covered them with gauze and secured the gauze with tape. After I'd done all that I wondered why I was so concerned about getting an infection when I was going to be dead soon anyway.

"You did good today," Ray said. "Better than any of us expected."

"Glad you think so. It feels like I went fifteen rounds with Muhammad Ali. And the day's still young."

"No, that's it for today. Two players are dead already, and that's the limit for a single day. You rest up for tomorrow, Number Eight. Lots more fun coming your way tomorrow."

"Tell me something," I said. "When do we get to meet the mysterious Number Nine?"

"It wouldn't be much of a mystery if I told you, now would it?"

"It's not much of a mystery anyway, because I already know who it is. It's Joe Crawford, isn't it? You motherfuckers are bring-ing my best friend into this. Let me tell you something. It's not going to work. I'm not going to fight him, so you might as well find someone else. I'll refuse to fight, and you'll have to zap me with the defibrillator. No drama in that. So find someone else for Number Nine. You hear me?"

No response. The audio on the G-29 went dead, which con-firmed my suspicions. Joe Crawford was going to be Number Nine. My only hope was that they would change it to someone else now that I knew.

I decided to use the rest of the day to figure out a way to find something to eat. I'd seen some blackberry bushes in the woods, and there were plenty of acorns on the ground, but I needed more than that to keep me strong for five days. I needed some sort of meat. I went outside and walked into the woods and tested a few branches from a few different types of trees. Most of them broke with little effort, but there was a sycamore that still had some spring in it. I cut a long, skinny branch and started tearing the leaves off. The leaves were brown and crunchy, but the branch still had some moisture in it from the summer. It still had some flexibility. I wanted to use it for a fishing pole, so I needed something that wasn't going to be too brittle. The sycamore branch seemed like it might fit the bill. After I tore the leaves off, I stripped the bark with my knife. The branch was about six feet long. One end was as fat as a handlebar grip, and it tapered down to the size of a pinky finger on the other end. I rubbed the entire length of it with handfuls of sand to get the sticky resin from the bark off. Now I had a pole, but I needed a line and a hook. And I would need some kind of lure.

I walked back to where I'd slain Number Five. The flies had already started on his wounds, and half a dozen buzzards circled overhead. It was against the rules to take weapons from a dead player, but nobody ever said anything about body parts. I thought I might be able to carve some hooks from his bones, slice off some strips of his flesh for bait. He was dead. I couldn't hurt him any more than I already had. If things were reversed, he would probably do the same to me. A guy who would kill his own brother probably wouldn't have a problem desecrating the corpse of a stranger.

I knelt down and held his left hand and stretched his arm out and pressed the knife blade against the underside of his wrist. I figured the bones in his hand would be best for fashioning fishhooks. Or maybe I needed something bigger. Maybe I should take the whole arm, or maybe even a leg. More meat on a leg for bait and bigger bones to work with. I thought about opening his gut and excising the liver. Liver was good bait for catfish. Catfish love liver.

I lifted the blade from his wrist and pressed it against his upper thigh. He was very muscular, so it was going to take some work to get the leg off. I took a deep breath. Before I started sawing, I looked at his face and his open eyes staring grayly out at nothing.

"I'm sorry," I said. "I'm sorry I had to kill you, and I'm sorry I have to chop you up now."

I said the words and then I dropped the knife and just stood there. I couldn't do it. I couldn't butcher this kid. He hadn't done anything wrong. His only sin was being in the wrong place at the wrong time, like me and all the other players. He had parents and grandparents and siblings and friends and coworkers who all loved him, and I couldn't cut him up no matter how much I needed to. It was only the first day, and I'd already been reduced to some sort of subhuman. I wasn't going to do it. I would starve to death before I gave Freeze the satisfaction.

I put the knife back in its sheath, grabbed my pole, and walked back toward my house.

Chapter Twenty-Two

I picked up some rocks on the way, a round one about the size of my fist and a flat one the size of a dinner plate. I had an idea. I pried up one of the floorboards at the edge of the porch with my survival knife and worked it up and down until the two sixteen-penny framing nails securing it were halfway exposed. I was glad they had used nails instead of screws. If they had used screws, I wouldn't have been able to pry them out with the knife. I would have been screwed.

Once the nails were halfway exposed, I banged on them with the round rock until they curled over the lip of the porch. Now the nails were J-shaped. Now the nails were hooks. I got underneath the heads and pounded them with the rock until they popped free. I picked one up and started grinding the sharp end against the edge of the flat stone. I ground the rust and oxidation off until it was shinier than new. I kept at it until the hooked end of the nail was flat and sharp, and I even filed a little barb into the tip. I did one nail and then the other. It took me over an hour, but when I finished I had two shiny silver nails that looked like oversized fishhooks with heads on the ends instead of eyelets.

Now that I had hooks, I needed some line. I needed string. There was a drawstring on the sleeping bag, but it wasn't going to be long enough. I thought about tying the drawstring and both my boot laces together, but then I got a better idea. I opened the cabinet under the sink, reached in, and grabbed the spool of dental floss. It was a generic grocery store brand, mint-flavored and waxed. I hadn't been using it, so it was still a full spool. Fifty-five yards. I reeled off twenty feet or so.

I didn't know if it was strong enough to use for fishing line or not. I needed to test it. I put the big flat rock and the fist-sized round rock in my backpack. I figured the pack weighed about ten pounds with the rocks in it. I tied the floss to one of the straps and tried to lift the backpack with it, but the floss broke. I wanted something that would withstand at least ten pounds in case I caught a decent-sized catfish. I knew I would be fishing for catfish, because nothing else in the freshwater pond would be big enough to gobble one of my makeshift hooks. I doubled the floss and tried lifting the backpack with it again, and this time it held. Now I was in business. I reeled out the entire spool and doubled it. I wrapped it around the end of my sycamore pole a bunch of times and tied it tightly, and then wrapped it around one of the hooks and tied that end off. Now I had a six-foot fishing pole with about thirty feet of line and a hook. I looked at the contraption and laughed. I was proud of it.

I was ready to walk to the pond and try it out, but I needed some bait. Catfish are bottom feeders. They'll eat almost anything. My stepfather used to use chicken livers. The bloodier and stinkier the better. I didn't have any chicken livers. If I'd had some, I probably would have eaten them myself. I didn't have anything. I decided to walk on down there and see what I could find.

I wrapped the line around the pole so it wouldn't get tangled. Walked outside and looked at my compass, headed into the woods in the direction of the pond. I was hoping I might run across a dead squirrel or a bird or something on my way down there, but no such luck.

It was almost three o'clock in the afternoon when I made it to the pond. It had taken me forty minutes to walk there, so I knew it would take that long to get back to the house. I needed to watch the time because I didn't want to get stuck in the woods after dark.

The bank around the pond was muddy and difficult to walk through. My boots were going to need a good cleaning when I got back to the house. There was a bullfrog sitting on a cypress stump and I tried to sneak up on it, thinking I would catch it and use it for fish bait. But it heard me and jumped away before I even got close. I was thinking about going farther up on the bank and digging for worms when I saw a dead bream floating near the stump the frog had jumped from. I waded into the water a couple of feet, reached over the stump, and grabbed the dead fish. It hadn't been dead long. Nothing had been nibbling on it, and it didn't smell much worse than a live fish. If it had been a little bigger, I might have taken it home for dinner. But it was small. Too small to eat, but fine for catfish bait. I carried it up to firmer ground, cut its head off, and gutted it and threaded it onto my hook.

I cast into an area clear of brush and fallen logs, knowing that if my hook got snagged and my line broke that would be it for fishing. I'd used all the dental floss, and I didn't have anything else that would work for line. I stood on the bank in the mud and waited, jiggling the pole now and then to stir my lure from the bottom of the pond. I stood there for an hour and didn't get any bites. The sun was getting low in the sky. I was about to pack it in and head back to the house when the line went taut. I wrapped the floss around my right arm and started backing away from the bank. Whatever had swallowed the hook was putting up a good fight. The floss was digging into my skin and I thought it was going to break. I kept wrapping it around my arm and backing up, and finally I landed the fish and it flopped around furiously in the mud until I walked back down and stabbed it in the brain with my knife. It was a fairly large catfish, about eighteen inches long and maybe three or four pounds. It was all I needed. I wrapped the line around the pole and picked the fish up with the knife still through its skull. When I turned to head back to the house there were two red jerseys standing in my way.

Chapter Twenty-Three

It was Number One and Number Three. The insurance salesman from Waterloo, Iowa, and the radiologist from Quincy, Illinois. They stood on the slight elevation above the pond's muddy bank, looking down on me with their arms folded over their chests.

I remembered from their bios that Number One held a second-degree black belt in tae kwon do and that Number Three played soccer in a corporate league. They were both slim and trim and in excellent physical condition. Neither of them appeared to have taken a beating the way I had. Neither of them appeared to be injured.

"That's a big fish," Number One said. "More than enough to share. Wouldn't you say so, Number Three?"

"Yeah. It's a nice one. Mind if we join you for dinner?"

Number One held a billy club in his left hand, and there was a coiled bullwhip hanging from his right shoulder. Those looked formidable enough, but Number Three had hit the weaponry jackpot. Number Three had the stun baton. Eight hundred thousand volts of hot electrical current bottled up in a wand the size of an eggbeater. Just waiting to be unleashed on some unlucky

player. I couldn't see Number Three's second weapon, but the
sight of the stun baton was enough to make my pulse quicken.
One stroke with that and you'd be down for the count.

Ray had told me over the G-29 that we were done for the day,
that two deaths were the limit, but I didn't trust him. I didn't trust
anyone involved in any of this lunacy. I half expected the alarm
to sound any second and for play to resume. It wouldn't have surprised me at all. If the alarm did sound, my only chance was to
run. My boots were heavily caked with mud and there were two
of them and they were faster than me. If the alarm sounded to
resume play, I was going to die.

"Sorry, but I already have plans for dinner," I said. "Maybe
some other time."

Number Three took a step toward me. "Give me the fucking
fish," he said.

"Yeah," Number One said. "Give him the fucking fish."

I had no intentions of giving them the fucking fish.

"I see how it is," I said. "Two against one. You guys are a team
now, huh? Fuck you. You can't have this fish. The only place this
fish is going is home with me to my house. Then it's going in my
belly. If you guys are hungry, maybe you could just run on down
to KFC and get yourselves a bucket of the colonel's original recipe. Eleven herbs and spices. And don't forget the Pepsi."

"Quite the smart-ass, aren't you?" Number One said. "That's
right. We're a team now. And you're going to be our first kill."

"Maybe you boys didn't get the memo, but play has been
suspended for the day. So run along now. It's getting dark, and
the streetlights will be coming on soon. Your mommies will be
worried."

Number One stuffed the nightstick into the waistband of
his pants, pulled the bullwhip from his shoulder, and lashed it
toward me. It cracked a few inches from my hand. He was good
with it. He must have had some experience. Or maybe he'd been

practicing with it all day. On his second try, the braided leather end wrapped around my catfish, and Number One gave the whip a quick jerk and the fish flew off the knife blade and up the bank toward him. Number Three bent over and picked it up.

"Give it back," I said. "I caught it fair and square. It's mine."

"And we stole it fair and square," Number One said. "Later, loser."

They walked away. There was nothing I could do. They walked away with my dinner and I couldn't do a damn thing about it. Even if the game had been on, it would have been stupid for me to fight them. Just like the bullies at school who used to beat me up in the bathroom and steal my milk money every day. They were bigger and stronger and faster than me, and there were two of them. And Number Three had the stun baton. It would have been useless to initiate a confrontation, even if the game had been on.

I thought about trying to catch another fish, but I didn't have anything for bait and it was getting dark. If I didn't get a move on soon, I was going to be spending the night in the woods. Spending the night in the cold, damp, gator-infested swamp wasn't much of an option. Something to avoid if at all possible.

"Hey," Number Three shouted from a hundred feet away. "If you're hungry, maybe you could just run on down to KFC and get yourself a bucket of the colonel's original recipe. Eleven herbs and spices. And don't forget the Pepsi."

They had a good laugh as they disappeared into the dusk. At that moment, I was as angry as I'd ever been about anything. I was boiling. I could have ripped someone's face off with my bare hands. It reminded me of the time in sixth grade when the bullies went too far. My stepfather never bought me enough clothes, and he never kept up with laundering the things I did have. I wore the same wrinkled shirt for a week sometimes and I never had a cool haircut or cool sneakers, and I became a regular source of amusement for a pair of degenerates in my sixth-grade class named

Kenny and Calvin. I was on the free lunch program, but the free lunch didn't include milk for some reason. You had to bring a nickel in every day if you wanted milk. My stepfather didn't give a shit if I had milk or not. He never gave me the money, but there was a very kind bus driver named Mr. Burkhart who knew I was poor and who discreetly handed me five cents every morning when I climbed into the bus. Then, at eleven o'clock every morning, after recess, Kenny and Calvin would beat me up in the bathroom and take the nickel Mr. Burkhart had so kindly given me. Beating me up and stealing my milk money was one thing, but the Monday we returned to school after Christmas break, Kenny and Calvin went too far. They took my money and then they forced me into one of the stalls and shoved my head into the toilet bowl. And the bowl wasn't clean. Calvin had taken a piss before they forced me in there, and he hadn't flushed. The bowl was full of Calvin's smelly urine, and they shoved my face right down into it. I thought those ignorant motherfuckers were going to drown me, and then a voice from outside the stall said, "Let him go."

Kenny and Calvin turned around. Through the water dripping from my forehead I saw Joe Crawford standing there outside the stall with his fists clenched. I knew Joe, but we ran with different crowds. Joe was from a good family. He always had clean clothes and he made good grades and he wasn't on the free lunch program. He had a cool haircut and cool sneakers and he never wore a dirty, wrinkled shirt to school. Frankly, I was surprised to see him there in the shitter after recess, taking up for the likes of me.

"Get out of here, Crawford," Kenny said. "This ain't none of your business."

"I'm making it my business. Now let him go before I kick your ass."

Calvin bolted out of the stall, cocked his fist, and swung at Joe's head, but Joe ducked and punched Calvin in the stomach and pushed him into the urine trough.

"You're dead, Crawford," Kenny said. He went for Joe, but I grabbed his foot and tripped him, and he fell face-first into the stall's metal doorframe. Bright red blood started gushing from his nose, and suddenly something happened to me. Suddenly I wasn't afraid of him anymore. I pushed him to the floor and straddled him and drove my fist into his face. I hit him with a right and then a left. Right, left, right, left. I thrashed him violently again and again until the bell rang for class to resume. The cacophonous clanging snapped me out of my superfocused rage and probably kept me from killing him. Joe and I walked out of the boys' room together and left the thugs there, one in a puddle of piss and the other in a puddle of blood.

Calvin and Kenny never went too far again.

From that day on, Joe Crawford and I were best friends. And from that day on, I didn't take any shit from anybody.

Now, because of me, Joe Crawford was going to be forced into the insanity of this game called Snuff Tag 9. There was little doubt in my mind Joe was going to be the ninth player. It sickened me. Joe was going to be forced into the game and more than likely lose his life, and I felt like it was all my fault. He never should have come to my rescue in sixth grade, the Monday we returned to school after Christmas break.

I wondered how Number One had gotten away with using his weapon during a time-out period. According to the rules, it was strictly prohibited. According to the rules, it was cause for immediate termination. Maybe it was because he hadn't actually touched me with it. He'd cracked the whip toward me, but it had only touched the fish. If Number One had been a few inches off with his aim and the whip had wrapped around my hand instead of the fish, he would probably be dead now. His defibrillator probably would have discharged and fried his heart. I wished that's what had happened. That's how furious I was. I wished a man had been executed for stealing my fish.

I started back toward my house. I tried to stomp some of the mud off my boots, and when that didn't work I scraped some off with my knife. It was a long walk and my feet were heavy and my legs were tired and I was hungry as hell. I hadn't eaten anything for nearly twenty-four hours.

I stopped for five minutes and picked some blackberries. I ate them as fast as I could pick them. The berries were bitter and the bushes were thorny and by the time I started walking again my hands were bleeding from all the scratches and my stomach hurt. I thought I was going to throw up, but I didn't. I stopped again and stuffed my pockets with acorns in the dying daylight, and when I finally made it to my house it was completely dark. I felt my way onto the porch and through the door and to the lamp on the little folding table by the cot. I switched on the lamp. A palmetto bug scurried across the floor, and I stomped it before it made it to safety. I wiped up the mess with a wad of toilet paper and threw the paper outside.

I remembered a scene from a prison movie where this guy was in solitary for a long time and resorted to eating cockroaches to stay alive. I wondered if I would ever get that hungry. Not in five days, I told myself. I sat on the floor and cracked a few of the acorns with the butt of my knife and ate them.

A voice came over the G-29. It wasn't Ray this time. It was Freeze.

"You let them take your fish," he said.

"I didn't exactly let them. They took it, and there wasn't much I could do to stop them. Play had already been suspended for the day, so I couldn't fight them. Anyway, I would have lost."

"Maybe. But I have to say, you surprised me today, Number Eight. I figured you were going to be one of the casualties, but you surprised me. Congratulations. Well done."

I didn't feel like congratulations were in order. I didn't feel like much of a winner. Two men had died for no reason. Tomorrow maybe two more would die. For no reason. For the amusement of a billionaire psychopath. It made me sick.

"Thanks a lot," I said. "How about sending me some sort of prize? A hamburger or something. Hell, I'd be happy to get my catfish back."

"How were you planning to cook the fish, if you had made it home with it?"

"Oh, you know. A little salt and pepper, butter and lemon, maybe some scallions and a light wine sauce."

"You're funny, Number Eight. I'll be sorry to see you go. I doubt you'll last another day. But really, how were you planning to cook the fish?"

"I don't know. I guess I would have tried to start a fire somehow. And if I hadn't been able to start a fire, I guess I would have eaten it raw. That's how hungry I am. What difference does it make? I'm sure as hell not going to be cooking anything now."

"Are you hungry enough to go out in the night and try to get your catch back?"

The question caught me by surprise. I hadn't even considered doing that.

"I don't have any idea where those punks are," I said. "I wouldn't know where to begin looking for their houses."

"I could lead you to them."

"You want me to navigate the swamp in the dark? It would be a suicide mission. No thanks."

He paused. "I could force you to go, but I won't. I'll leave it up to you this time. If you want to go, I'll have a flashlight brought to you and I'll lead you every step of the way. If you're successful, you can even keep the flashlight. And, as a bonus, I'll supply you with a butane cigarette lighter for the rest of the week. You'll be able to start a fire and cook your fish tonight, and you'll be able to start fires and cook all your meals for the duration of the game.

For as long as you keep winning, that is. Think about it, Number Eight."

I thought about it. Freeze wanted some more drama for the day. He wasn't satisfied with the two deaths. He wanted more action. He was a junkie for it. He knew how angry I was about losing the fish, and he wanted to capitalize on that emotion. He wanted to catch it on camera. Another scene for his depraved film. I didn't want to give him the satisfaction, but I wanted my fish back. And I wanted that cigarette lighter. And the flashlight. Having the lighter and the flashlight would improve my chances of survival. Still, I would have to go up against Number One and Number Three. Two of them against one of me. I would have to go up against them on their own turf, in the dark. I didn't stand a chance in hell. It was a suicide mission, like I'd said before.

"All right," I said. "I'll do it."

Chapter Twenty-Four

Half an hour later, someone knocked. I got up off my cot and answered the door. It was a man wearing blue coveralls and a red ball cap. He looked very young. He looked like he should have been bagging groceries somewhere.

"I brought you this," he said.

He handed me a black metal flashlight. I switched it on. It worked.

"What about the butane lighter?" I said.

"This is all I have."

"All right. Thanks."

He turned and disappeared into the darkness. I shut the door and sat back down on the cot. Freeze had told me to wait for instructions. I waited. I got up and washed my boots off in the sink and cleaned the scratches on my hands with peroxide. I waited some more. I was lying on the bed and was about to doze off when Freeze's voice came over the G-29.

"I want you to leave your house and walk northeast," he said.

"What about the lighter?" I said. "Some kid brought me a flashlight, but no lighter. That was part of the deal."

"You'll get it after. Leave your house and walk northeast. Now, please."

I got up and walked outside. Switched the flashlight on, looked at my compass, headed northeast.

The sky was overcast. No moon, no stars. I turned the flashlight off for a second, just to see how dark it was without it. I couldn't see my hand in front of my face. It would have been impossible to navigate without a light source. I didn't know how far I was going to have to go, but I hoped the batteries would last. If the batteries died, I would be stuck in the swamp until morning.

I looked at my compass again and continued northeast. I continued at a steady pace for twenty minutes or so.

"How much farther?" I said.

No response.

The rules stated that play usually began at sunrise and ended at sunset. Usually. But it was becoming increasingly obvious that Freeze modified the rules ad lib as the game progressed. The rules were whatever struck his fancy at the moment. Right now play was supposedly suspended for the night. But here I was on my way to another player's house. Number One's or Number Three's. Wherever they'd taken the fish. I had to expect play to resume at some point.

Number One and Number Three wouldn't be expecting me. I had the element of surprise on my side. Unless Freeze had told them I was on the way. That was a possibility. Maybe the whole thing was a setup. Maybe Number One and Number Three would be lying in wait and the alarm would sound and play would resume and Number Three would zap me with that stun baton and that would be it. Freeze had made it sound like he was on my side, like he wanted me to get the fish back. But maybe he had led Number One and Number Three to me in the first place. Maybe that whole scene at the pond had been orchestrated as well. Now I wished I hadn't agreed to going out. I wished I'd stayed in my house where it was safe. I'd allowed pride to get the best of me. I wasn't even very hungry anymore. The hunger pains had subsided. They'd faded to a dull ache just below my left rib cage.

This whole thing was pointless. I'd been seduced by the carrot Freeze had dangled, by the flashlight and butane lighter. And I'd been seduced by my own past. I was chasing the ghosts of Calvin and Kenny. That's what was really going on here, and it was stupid.

"I've changed my mind," I said. "You hear me, Freeze? I've decided not to do this. Fuck that fish. I'll catch another one tomorrow."

I looked at my compass, turned, and headed back in the direction of my house.

"Not so fast," Freeze said. "We made a deal, and you have to keep your end of it. You can't just bail on a whim. We have a contract. There's no turning back now."

"You said it was up to me."

"Originally it was. You could have said no, and that would have been that. You could have turned your light off and gone to sleep and waited for play to resume in the morning. You could have done that, but you said yes to my proposal. Now you're going to stick to it."

"And if I don't?"

"Are you forgetting about the defibrillator wired to your heart? I could snap my fingers and have you executed in a nanosecond."

"But you won't," I said. "It's day one, and you're already down to six players. You need me to stick around for at least another day or two. You need me for the game."

I continued walking toward my house. I was testing him, trying to see exactly how much I could get away with.

"So you're calling my bluff?" Freeze said.

"Yeah. I'm calling your bluff. Go ahead and kill me if you want to. I'm going home."

There was a brief pause, and then Freeze said, "You're right, Number Eight. I was bluffing. I do need you around for a bit longer. But guess what? I can give you things, like the flashlight and the lighter, but I can also take things away. How would you like it if I shut the water off in your house? I think I'll start with that. Then, if you fail to cooperate again, I'll take one of your weapons away. Then—"

"I get the point," I said. "All right. You win."

Of course he won. He always won.

Freeze was not only an action junkie, he also had some sort of god complex. He enjoyed having total control over people. You could feel it in the way he spoke, in his attitude. He was a billionaire. He had everything money could buy, but it wasn't enough for him to own things. He had to own people. He was like a third-world dictator to the nth degree. Freeze giveth, and Freeze taketh away. With the Snuff Tag 9 game, it was like he was buying his way to the status of deity. The players basically had no choice but to obey. If we didn't obey, he would make us suffer. Or he would make our loved ones suffer. Any resistance was an exercise in futility. In this massive theater of depravity he'd created, Freeze was omnipotent. He was in total control.

I looked at the compass again and turned back northeast.

"Glad you decided to see it my way," he said. "I want you to turn due east now. You're almost there."

I did as instructed and turned due east. I cupped my left hand over the flashlight to muffle its brightness. Freeze said I was almost there. I didn't want Number One and Number Three to see me coming. Unshielded, the flashlight would have been like a beacon. I cupped my left hand over it and saw the hardware holding my bones together. Six surgeries in two years. Six surgeries, and the range of motion in my hand still wasn't anywhere near what it was before a piece of shit hillbilly dishwasher in Tennessee named Lester stomped it with the heel of his boot. I could grip things all right, but I couldn't flatten my palm out all the way. And trying to press a guitar string against a fret sent white-hot jolts of pain from my fingertips to my jawbone. Lester had made sure my hand was never going to work right again. Lester was six feet under now, but in a way he'd beaten me. He'd robbed me of ever playing music again. I thought about Lester sometimes, and every time I did I hoped the son of a bitch was rotting in hell.

Through the trees I saw a faint glimmer of light ahead. As I got closer, I could see that the glow was coming from the window of a house identical to mine. I switched off the flashlight and crept to within a hundred feet of the place. Number One and Number Three were outside. I could see their silhouettes in front of the shack. They were on their knees beside a pile of twigs. One of them appeared to be feverishly twirling a stick against something on the ground.

"I thought you said you knew how to do this," Number One said. "I'm about to eat that damn catfish raw."

"Fuck you. I'm not eating a raw fish. I'll throw it in the woods for the raccoons before that happens." He paused. "This shit worked when I was a Boy Scout, so I don't know what the fuck is up. Maybe it's the wrong kind of wood, or it's not dry enough or something. You want to give it a try?"

Number Three offered the stick to Number One.

"I have a better idea," Number One said. "Let's use your stun gun."

"Huh?"

"Sure, man. Aim it at the pile of sticks and let 'er rip. The spark from the electrical discharge should get the fire going."

"I don't know. That's one shot. Then it'll take at least three hours to charge back up. That's three hours I'll be without my weapon. And it might not even work."

"Play's suspended for the day anyway. You don't need your weapon right now. I'm telling you, it's our best chance at starting a fire."

"I don't know. I'd feel better about trying it if we had some sort of accelerant. A pill bottle full of gasoline or something."

Number One stood up. "Hell yeah!" he said. "You just gave me another idea. A great idea. My brother's a cop, so I know a little about pepper spray. That shit's alcohol based, man. Flammable as hell. I'll just tear a little piece from the sheet on my bed and you can douse it with pepper spray and tuck it under the kindling and zap it with the stun gun. That should get some flames going for sure."

"You want me to use both my weapons?" Number Three said.

"You don't have to use all the pepper spray. One squirt should do the trick. Then you can just charge the stun baton while we sleep and it'll be a hundred percent ready for tomorrow. So really you're not losing anything except a little Mace, and we'll be able to eat a nice hot supper. Trust me. This is going to work."

Number Three stood. He threw the stick he'd been twirling onto the pile of kindling on the ground and said, "All right. Let's give it a try."

Chapter Twenty-Five

Number One walked into the house and came back out holding a white piece of fabric, a corner torn from one of his bedsheets. I wondered if his idea would work. It sounded feasible in theory. I stood there quietly and watched.

Number One tucked the piece of fabric under some of the kindling on the ground. "Now shoot it with some of that pepper spray," he said.

Number Three pulled the canister from one of the flap pockets on his pants. He backed up several feet, aimed, and shot. The sparkling liquid ejected in a steady stream.

Number Three squirted the fabric for a second or two and then returned the canister to his pocket.

"You think that's enough?" he said.

"Should be," Number One said. "Go ahead and hit it with the stun gun and see what happens."

Number Three pulled the stun baton from his waistband. "I've never used one of these things before."

"My brother had to get zapped by one as part of his training at the police academy. Said it hurts like a bitch. Said there's no way a guy's going to take a shot from that and get up and run away. Even works on those crazy motherfuckers jacked up on crystal meth and shit."

"All right. Here goes nothing."

Number Three leaned over and shot the piece of bedsheet with the stun baton. A blue bolt of electrical current arced from the tip, and a bright orange flame danced up from the fabric immediately. Number One and Number Three quickly started scooting the pile of twigs over the flame and then tossed some larger branches over the kindling from a stack off to the side. A few seconds later the wood started crackling and a white plume of smoke rose skyward.

"Success!" Number One shouted. He danced a little celebratory jig.

"I have to hand it to you," Number Three said. "It was a good idea. Worked like a charm. I'm just going to go in and put this thing on the charger."

"All right. I'll get supper going."

They both walked into the house. While they were inside, I took the opportunity to move a little closer. I got to within fifty feet of the house before they came back outside. Number One was holding a stainless steel skillet identical to the one at my place, and Number Three was holding a roll of toilet paper.

Apparently Number Three needed to take a shit.

"I'll be right back," he said.

"All right."

Number One walked to the fire and held the skillet over it. Neither of them had a knife, so I wondered how they had cleaned the catfish. Then I saw it in the pan. The head was still on it, and so was the tail, but the belly had been split open and butterflied. I reckoned one of them had slit it with a sharp rock or something and had scooped its guts out by hand. That's what I would have done, if I hadn't had a knife.

The catfish sizzled in its own juices, and in a couple of minutes the air was filled with its aroma. It smelled heavenly. I could have eaten the entire thing by myself with no problem. But I didn't really care that much about the fish anymore. I wanted something else. I wanted the stun baton. It was in the house on the charger, unguarded at the moment. The rules stated you couldn't take a weapon from a dead player. When a player dies, his weapons die with him. But the rules didn't say anything about taking a weapon from a living player. The rules didn't say anything about it, and I didn't feel compelled to follow a rule that wasn't there.

I wanted that stun baton.

Play was still suspended, so I couldn't charge in and fight my way inside the house. I didn't want to do that anyway. Even if play were to resume, and even if the alarm sounded to allow knives and nunchucks and bullwhips and nightsticks and chains and pepper spray and stun guns and slingshots and brass knuckles and fifty-caliber blowguns with three darts, the odds were against me. Even with Number Three's best weapon temporarily out of commission. I couldn't fight my way in. I needed to do it the stealthy way. I needed to sneak in and take the stun baton and escape unnoticed.

Number Three returned from his trip to the woods. He took the toilet paper inside, clomped back off the porch, and stood beside Number One. He peered into the skillet.

"You think it's done?" he said.

"I don't know," Number One said. "I ain't no Emeril Lagasse."

He pronounced Emeril's last name La-*gassy*.

"It smells done," Number Three said. "Let's eat."

"All right. You want to take it inside?"

"Kind of stuffy in there. I say we sit outside on the deck."

"All right."

Number One carried the steaming skillet to the porch. Number Three followed. They sat across from each other

Indian-style with the skillet between them. They let the fish cool for a few minutes and then started pinching off pieces of the white flesh with their fingers.

"This is good," Number Three said. "Lots of bones, but it's good."

"Yeah. Did you see the look on Number Eight's face when I snatched it away from him with the bullwhip? Priceless."

"That was some trick, all right. Where did you learn to use a whip like that?"

Before Number One answered, I switched the flashlight on and off a few times in quick succession, as if trying to signal with it.

Number One rose abruptly. "Did you see that?"

"What?" Number Three said.

"I saw a flash of light out of the corner of my eye. Out there in the woods."

"I didn't see anything. Maybe it was one of the cameras or something."

"Maybe. I'm going to go check it out."

Number Three continued eating. "Chill out. I'm sure it was nothing. Might have been your imagination playing tricks on you. You said you didn't get any sleep last night. Sleep deprivation can cause minor hallucinations like that sometimes. I had a patient who—"

"Bullshit. There it is again. Someone's out there. Someone's fucking with us."

Number Three stood. "Yeah. I saw it that time."

"Who's out there?" Number One shouted.

I didn't respond. I picked up a rock and threw it into the woods on the other side of the house.

"What was that?" Number Three said. "It came from over there."

"Must be more than one of them. Another couple of players must have teamed up. We need to run them off or they'll be fucking with us all night." He paused. "How in the hell did they find your house, anyway?"

"How in the hell should I know?"

"Maybe you told someone before you hooked up with me. Maybe you're in cahoots with *them*. Maybe they're going to wait in the woods till morning and then y'all are going to gang up and kill my ass. Well, fuck you. I'm going home, ace. I'm going back to my own house."

Number One was getting paranoid, another symptom of sleep deprivation and extreme stress. If someone were predisposed to delusions, Snuff Tag 9 could certainly flush that trait to the surface. Number One was predisposed to delusions. Number One was losing it. He reached into the skillet, broke off approximately half of the catfish, and stalked off the porch.

"You'll never find your house in the dark," Number Three said. "You need to stay here tonight. Like we planned. I promise you I'm not in cahoots with anyone else."

Number One stopped by the fire and looked at his compass. "Oh, I'll find it all right. I know exactly where it is. And the game's over for the day. The motherfuckers in the woods can't touch me right now."

"What about our agreement?"

"You go to hell. That's what about it."

Number One disappeared into the woods.

"You're making a big mistake," Number Three shouted. He shrugged and sat back down to his dinner. He didn't seem worried that someone was in the woods watching him.

I wanted him to worry. I wanted him to know I was still here. I did the thing with the flashlight again. Number Three stood up again.

"Who's there?" he said.

I crept to my right, along the perimeter of the woods, inching closer to the clearing as I went. I could see Number Three, but he couldn't see me. The fire was crackling loudly, so I doubted he could hear me either. He pulled the canister of pepper spray from his flap pocket and walked toward the position I had last flashed the light from. I didn't know what he was thinking. Play was suspended, and weapons weren't allowed. If he shot me with the Mace, he would be terminated immediately. No questions asked. That was the rule.

I briefly entertained the notion of running toward him with my knife raised overhand. That might freak him out, I thought. Might make him panic enough to hit me with the pepper spray. If he hit me with the pepper spray, Freeze would hit him with the defibrillator. Game over. I briefly entertained the notion, but then dismissed it. Number Three was no dummy. He'd probably pulled the spray *hoping* whoever was in the woods showed his hand. He had no intention of actually using it. It was a ruse. A bluff. A decoy. He kept walking toward my former position, and I kept walking away from it. Closer and closer to the edge of the clearing.

The gap between us widened. I knew he wouldn't go very far into the woods. Too dark. Once he got away from the light of the fire, he wouldn't be able to see where he was going. I knew he wouldn't go very far into the woods, so I needed to time my move just right.

"Who's there?" Number Three said again. He'd walked past the threshold, beyond the clearing, and into the brush a few feet. I estimated his position from the sound of his voice. I couldn't see him anymore. I counted off five seconds, hoping he was still moving away from the house, and then made my dash.

"Son of a bitch," Number Three shouted.

He saw me. He started running back toward the house. I had a head start, but he was faster than me. It was going to be close. Too close for comfort. I thought about turning around and running back into the woods. But if he caught me, what could he do? Nothing. Play was suspended. Fighting wasn't allowed. All he could do was beat me to the house and protect his property. Unless the alarm sounded to resume play. If the alarm sounded, we would have to fight it out. I decided to go for it anyway. My primary objective was to stay alive for four more days. In order for that to happen, six more people would have to die. The stun baton would be a huge help toward achieving my primary objective. I wanted it. I needed it. I had to have it.

I kept running toward the house.

Number Three kept running toward the house.

I made it onto the porch, darted inside, and snatched the stun baton and the charging cable from the wall socket. Through the window I saw Number Three stampeding past the fire, all six five and two hundred ten pounds of him. When his feet hit the porch planks, I slammed the door with all the force I could muster. He went crashing into it with a solid thud. I heard him stumble backward. I heard him fall.

I opened the door and jumped over him and bent down and grabbed the remaining catfish from the skillet and ran like the wind and didn't look back.

The alarm never sounded.

Chapter Twenty-Six

I stuffed the stun gun and the charging cord into one of my flap pockets. Held the fish in one hand, nibbling on it as I walked, and the flashlight in the other. The flashlight's batteries were dying. The bulb grew dimmer and dimmer as I trudged along.

A few minutes into my hike, Freeze spoke to me over the G-29.

"You came very close to breaking a cardinal rule, Number Eight. Do you know what happens when you break a cardinal rule? Immediate termination. It's a judgment call, but what you did to Number Three could possibly be interpreted as an engagement in combat. Play was suspended at the time, and of course any physical confrontation was a big no-no. I'm holding a remote control in my hand right now. If I push the red button, your defibrillator will discharge and your heart will stop beating. It's a judgment call, and I'm the judge."

"And the jury and the executioner," I said. "I know the rules, Freeze. You don't need to remind me. I never touched the guy."

"You never touched him, but you did something that caused him to be knocked out."

"It was an accident."

He laughed. "Whatever. Anyway, I've decided to allow you to continue for now. And I have to say, that was quite a score. You walked away with the stun baton and half the catfish. Congratulations."

"Thanks. Yeah, it's been a banner first day for me."

"You've surprised me. I never expected you to be so clever, so fearless. You might actually be a dark horse in this competition. You might actually stand a chance."

"I got lucky. That's all. So since I'm still alive, I'm assuming it was OK for me to steal Number Three's stun baton."

"This is the first time something like this has happened. An unprecedented occurrence. There's nothing written about taking a weapon from a player who's still alive, so it wouldn't be fair to penalize you for doing it. But I will address it in next year's edition of the rule book. Snuff Tag Nine is ever-evolving. That's part of the beauty of it. Every year new things come up, and new rules are written. I just love it. It's so perfect, don't you think?"

Perfect for a capricious sadistic monster like you, I thought.

"Sure," I said. "Perfect. Hey, you think you could send your courier around with some fresh batteries? This thing's dying."

"Batteries weren't part of the deal," he said. "I promised you a flashlight. You're lucky it came with the first set of batteries. If you want more, you'll have to earn them."

"What about my cigarette lighter?"

"It's on your bed. You'll find it when you get to your house."

"Is the butane included, or will I have to earn that too?"

"Don't be a smart-ass, Number Eight. I'm signing off for the night. Ta-ta. See you in the morning, bright and early."

"Later," I said.

The flashlight had become practically useless, but the sky had cleared and the moon was out and I could see well enough to navigate. By the time I made it to my house, I had eaten most of the catfish.

I was still hungry.

The half I'd snatched from Number Three's skillet happened to be the half with the head on it, so I thought I might be able to boil it and make a stew.

The butane lighter was on my bed as promised. There was a handwritten note under it.

Dear Number Eight,

There is enough fuel in this lighter for approximately ten ignitions, lasting approximately three seconds each. Use sparingly, or your butane will soon be gone. Of course, the lighter will probably last longer than you will regardless. Joking! A little ST9 humor for you.

All Best,

Freeze

What a douche bag. I should have known he wouldn't give me a lighter full of fuel. So I had ten lights. I could deal with that. It was like having ten matches. Beat the hell out of what I had before, which was nothing. Even though I had to risk my life for it.

And I had the stun baton now. That was the prize I valued most. Number One and Number Three had started a fire with it, but they'd had alcohol from the pepper spray as an accelerant. I doubted a spark from the baton would start a fire on its own, although I would certainly give it a try if the occasion arose. I plugged it in so it would have a full charge by morning.

I opened the cabinet under the sink and took out the stainless steel skillet. I ran some water in it and lowered the catfish carcass with the head on it into the water. I went out and gathered some sticks and branches and dry leaves and started a fire about twenty feet from my porch. I gathered some of the wild onions growing in the clearing, washed them in the sink, and added them to the skillet. I needed some sort of platform to set the skillet on. It would take a while for the water to boil and the onions and fish head to stew, and I didn't want to kneel by the fire and hold the skillet that long. I wasn't even sure I was able. I was exhausted.

The cot in my room was composed of an aluminum frame topped with a thin mattress. I pulled the mattress off, and under it was a pattern of steel wire supports that served as springs. I decided to use that for my grill. I left the mattress and linens on the floor and pulled the frame outside and positioned it over the fire. I set the skillet on the wire supports and stood back and marveled at my ingenuity.

It took about ten minutes for the water to start boiling, but when it did it bubbled furiously and I had to keep adding to it to prevent it from drying up. I let the fish and onions cook for about thirty minutes, stirring the mixture occasionally with my survival knife. When the catfish's skull got soft enough I sliced into it and allowed its contents to drain out into the soup. I plucked the eyeballs out, watched them bob on the surface like a couple of glassy black garbanzo beans.

I took the skillet off the fire and let it cool a while. I didn't have a spoon to eat with, so I used the plastic top to my shaving cream can. I dipped out a cupful and tasted it, got an eyeball on the first slurp. It was chewy, like a piece of squid or a chicken gizzard. It tasted OK. It could have used some salt, but the onions added a wild tang to it. I sat on the porch and ate all of it and then tossed the bones in the woods and extinguished the fire and washed the skillet in the sink and went to bed on the floor. I fell asleep immediately, and immediately I went reeling into a horrifying dream featuring The Potato Man.

He was the size of a regular potato, but he had a face and arms and legs. I started having recurring nightmares about him when I was in second grade. He would chase me around the house, snapping at me with those thick, horselike teeth, and he would always say something cryptic or profound that I couldn't quite process when I woke up.

For the past year or so The Potato Man had returned. He was making frequent appearances again, and he was every bit as frightening to me at fifty as he was at seven.

In this one I was at my grandmother's house in Jeffersonville, Indiana, sitting at the kitchen table drinking a cup of coffee and smoking a cigarette. Gray and red tiles on the floor, shiny black skillet on the stove, chrome toaster and percolator on the counter. The back door was open, and through the storm door window I could see the birdfeeder on the porch. A bright red male cardinal stood there frantically feasting on sunflower seeds, making a mess with the hulls.

I felt content at my grandmother's house. I always felt safe there. In my dream I was in my early thirties and I had lost everything. My wife and daughter and band to a plane crash, all my money and worldly possessions to cocaine. I'd completely lost interest in music. I was in a dark place, confused about where to go or what to do. But I always felt safe and content at my grandmother's house, and I was sitting there alone enjoying my coffee and cigarette when The Potato Man darted out from the space between the stove and refrigerator. He looked at me with those runny bloodshot eyes and snarled at me with those thick yellow teeth, and I rose clumsily trying to get away and my coffee spilled on the red-and-white-checkered tablecloth and I ran, and suddenly I was in a long, dark hallway and I didn't have any clothes on. I ran and ran as fast as I could, but my muscles didn't want to cooperate. It was like trying to sprint underwater, and The Potato Man was nipping at my heels. I was stark naked and he was gaining on me, and then he started singing Johnny Cash's song "I Walk the Line." He sang the first verse, and then he shouted something that seemed totally unrelated. He shouted something, but he was behind me and his voice was muffled and I couldn't understand the words. He shouted again, and it sounded like he said *the change on the aloe fence* and it didn't make any sense and I woke up then dripping with sweat and my pulse pounding in my eardrums.

The change on the aloe fence. It was funny, in a nonsensical way. It made me laugh.

But it was still dark outside, and The Potato Man was an asshole, so I turned over and went back to sleep.

Chapter Twenty-Seven

The sun woke me up at around seven a.m. The alarm hadn't sounded to resume play. At least I hadn't heard it. I figured it would have woken me if it had sounded. It was harsh and unmistakable, like a goose honking into a microphone.

I drank some water from the lid of my shaving cream can. There wasn't a mirror at the sink, so I looked at my distorted reflection in my knife blade. There were cuts and abrasions and bruises on my face and two days' worth of stubble. I decided not to shave. I decided it would hurt too bad. I washed up and put my uniform on. I threaded the sheath for the knife through my belt and loaded the nunchucks in my right flap pocket along with the butane lighter. According to Freeze, I had fuel for nine more ignitions. I needed to keep that in mind and use the lighter sparingly. I took the stun baton off the charger and put it in my other flap pocket and pulled my boots on. I was ready to start the day.

I walked outside. It was only day two, and I already felt like I'd been hit by a truck. My feet were blistered and my hands were scratched and every muscle and joint in my body throbbed.

I needed coffee. I needed the caffeine. I felt edgy and I had a headache.

But it was a nice day. The sun was shining, and I figured it was about sixty degrees.

The ashes were still smoldering from the fire I'd started, and there was a blackened area on the bed frame's wire supports where I'd used them as a cooking surface. Birds chirped and squirrels scurried and the tangy smell of autumn in the swamp filled the air. Another day in paradise.

I stood on the porch and took some deep breaths, wondering if this would be my last morning. Wondering if I had it in me to struggle through another twenty-four hours of this insanity.

I was thinking about venturing into the woods to pick some blackberries for breakfast when the alarm sounded for play to resume. The game was on, but the alarm for weapons hadn't sounded yet. If I met another player right now, I would have to kill him with my bare hands. The way I felt at the moment, I didn't think it would be a problem. I always feel like killing someone before my first cup of coffee in the morning.

I waited for my instructions to come over the G-29. I waited for fifteen or twenty minutes, but all was quiet. I went inside and got another drink of water. Took the pillowcase off my pillow and went out to forage for some victuals.

I loaded up with blackberries and dandelion greens and wild onions and acorns. There were squirrels everywhere. I could hear them high in the trees, and occasionally one would scrabble down and grab a nut and go back up. I wanted to catch one and kill it. I could cook the meat and eat it and then use the organs for fish bait. I knew they were too quick for me to catch by hand, and I didn't have the materials to make a snare or a trap. I needed a rifle. Or a bow and arrow. I wondered if I could fashion a bow from a tree branch. Maybe, but the only string I had was the dental floss, and I didn't think that would work. It might work if I tripled or quadrupled it, but then I wouldn't have anything to fish with. Arrows would be easy enough to make. Or a spear. Of course. I could sharpen a tree branch and use it for a spear and kill as many squirrels as I wanted. I got excited thinking about it. I imagined it was the same feeling a prehistoric caveman had when he finally solved a perplexing problem. How to move a boulder out of the way with a lever or something. I felt like a genius.

The sycamore branch had worked well enough for the fishing pole, but I thought something stiffer and heavier might be better for a spear. I found a maple and broke one of the lower branches off and stripped the twigs. It felt good in my hands. The weight and balance felt right. I pulled out my knife and sat down and started whittling on the narrow end.

The ground was crunchy with leaves and pine needles. I'd always thought of swampland as being damp and mushy, but the Okefenokee was over four hundred thousand acres, and apparently the part Freeze owned was high and dry. The pond where I'd caught the catfish was the only water source I'd run across. Maybe it was the only water source on the entire playing field. I considered that as I shaved the end of my maple branch to a sharp point. If the pond was the only water source, then all the players would naturally gravitate toward it. They would try to catch fish and frogs and turtles and whatnot for food, and the odds of crossing paths with one or more of them on any given day were probably better than even. That made the pond a dangerous place to be. A place to avoid if possible, especially while the game was on.

Which reminded me the game was on now and that I needed to be hyperaware of my surroundings.

There were still six players, myself and five others. Five young able-bodied men who desperately wanted to see me dead. I took inventory: Number One, the insurance salesman from Waterloo, Iowa; Number Three, the radiologist from Quincy, Illinois; Number Four, the electrical engineer from Indianapolis,

Indiana; Number Six, the airline pilot from Louisville, Kentucky; and Number Seven, the diving instructor from Palatka, Florida. The former Navy SEAL.

And one to come, Number Nine, whose identity was yet unknown.

Number Two and Number Five were dead. Of the remaining players, I'd encountered Number One and Number Three. I hadn't met Number Four or Number Six or Number Seven yet. Maybe I wouldn't have to. Maybe they would die in battle before I got the chance. Then again, maybe I would be the one to die. Five people in relatively close proximity wanted that to happen. I tried not to think about it.

The woods were still and quiet. No wind. The birds had even stopped singing. There was an ominous vibe to it, like something was about to happen. I stood up and looked around, but I didn't see anything.

I decided my spear was sharp enough. I bunched up some leaves to use as a target, gave it a couple of practice throws into the pile. It flew straight and true. I'm a decent barroom dart player, so my aim wasn't bad. My arm felt good. I felt good. I felt like stripping naked and running through the woods with the spear and yelping at the top of my lungs. But I didn't. I found a nice spot by a stand of oak trees and crouched down and waited.

And waited.

It was as if the squirrels were aware of my presence now, aware that I had a new tool to skewer them with. Or maybe their breakfast time was over and they were taking naps in their nests. I'd seen dozens earlier, and now there were none. Just my luck, I thought. I nibbled on some berries and waited some more.

I heard some leaves rustling, and I turned and saw a man about fifty feet away wearing blue coveralls and a red ball cap. He was adjusting a camera mounted on a tree. It wasn't the guy who had brought me the flashlight, but he looked familiar. I'd seen him somewhere before. He finished what he was doing and turned to walk away. That's when he noticed me. He pulled the bill of his hat down and took off at a trot. He'd screwed up. I wasn't supposed to have seen him. I tried to think when and where we'd met previously, but I couldn't remember.

I sat there and waited on the squirrels some more. Finally, after I'd been in the same spot for over an hour, one of the crummy little bushy-tailed bastards cautiously descended the trunk. He came down in nervous increments, with a stiff tail and surveying eyes. He stopped at the base of the tree, where the roots met the ground. I was close enough to see his nostrils flaring. Our eyes locked and his muscles tensed and I stood and heaved the spear in one quick and fluid motion. My aim was way off, nearly two feet to the right, but he'd started to dart that way and the spear impaled him between the shoulders. He flopped up and fell to the ground and clawed the air a few times and then lay still.

I'd done it. I'd killed a squirrel. First try. I couldn't believe my good luck.

I walked to him and looked down. He wasn't dead yet. He was still twitching. I pulled my knife and slit his throat to put him out of his misery, and then I lifted him and carried him away on the end of the spear.

On the way home, a voice came over the G-29. A voice I hadn't heard before.

"Good morning, Number Eight."

"Good morning," I said.

"My name is Charles, and I'll be your guide today."

"OK."

"I see you've killed a squirrel."

"Yeah. My lucky day, huh?"

"In more ways than one. Since you killed another player yesterday, today is going to be a bye for you. You're not to engage with any of the remaining players, and they're not allowed to engage with you."

"I get the whole day off?" I said. "What's the catch?"

"No catch. Enjoy it, because tomorrow you'll be back in the fray."

I walked into the clearing where my house was located.

"Sounds good," I said. "So why do I need a guide if I'm not going to be playing?"

"I'll show you in a few minutes."

I set the dead squirrel and the spear and the pillowcase full of berries and onions and acorns on the porch and walked inside to get a drink of water.

Chapter Twenty-Eight

I drank two cups of water, sat on my mattress for a few minutes, and waited for Charles to come back on. When he didn't, I walked out to the porch and used my knife to skin and gut the squirrel. I'd never done it before, but I managed OK. I gathered some kindling and some large branches and used the butane lighter to start a fire. I cooked the entrails in the skillet to use for fish bait later. Raw would have been better, but I didn't want them to lie around and rot and I didn't have any ice or a refrigerator. I set the squirrel's carcass, minus the skin and head and guts, directly on the makeshift grill but not directly over the fire. I wanted it to roast slowly, over an hour or so. I scooted some hot embers under it, and occasionally a drop of fat would land with a sizzle and let me know it was cooking.

"Hello, Number Eight. It's me, Charles, again."

"Hello, Charles."

"I want you to go inside now. We have a surprise for you."

"I don't want to leave my meat unattended here. It might burn."

"It looks like it's cooking very slowly. It'll be fine. This won't take long."

I lifted the skillet and carried it to the house and left it and the steaming squirrel guts on the porch. The blob of organs and intestines actually smelled pretty good. I was tempted to eat it myself. I was very hungry.

I walked inside, and to my amazement there was a flat-screen television against the wall adjacent to my bed. It was fairly large, thirty-seven inches, I guessed.

"Where did this come from?" I said.

"From a recessed cavity under your floor. Nifty, eh? I accessed the motorized lift remotely. It's all closed circuit, so don't get any ideas about watching *Seinfeld* reruns or something tonight. Now, have a seat on your mattress there and enjoy the show. This is live, by the way. What you'll be watching is in real time."

I sat on the mattress and looked at the screen. Outside, I heard the alarm sound once and then three times in a row. The game was on, and weapons were allowed.

The video faded in.

Number One was walking through the woods. He heard the alarm sound, pulled out his nightstick. The bullwhip was looped and attached to his belt. He crept slowly through the brush, breathing heavily. Continuously looking left and right. Occasionally checking his back to make sure nobody was behind him. He reminded me of the squirrel. Hyperaware and ready to take action at a moment's notice.

The video cut to a harshly lit interior. There was a concrete floor with oil stains on it and a lawn mower draped with clear plastic and a Ping-Pong table folded up and rolled to the side. It was the inside of a residential garage. It was the room I'd seen on video before, where they'd beheaded Nathan Broadway. A new man was sitting in the middle of the room, strapped to a wooden chair with duct tape. There was a black hood over his head.

Otherwise he was naked. There was a Japanese samurai sword mounted on the wall several feet behind him.

The video cut back to Number One stalking through the woods. I could see how this was going to go. It was going to cut back and forth between the interior scene and the exterior scene. They were going to show me two murders occurring simultaneously. I didn't want to watch either one of them. I didn't want to, but I couldn't turn away.

Number One came to a clearing. In the middle of the clearing, there was a house identical to mine. The camera zoomed in on the porch. There was a brass 3 tacked to one of the supports. It was Number Three's house. I'd been inside it yesterday when I stole the stun baton. Number One and Number Three had been partners yesterday, and now they were going to be forced to battle. Number One had two weapons, the nightstick and the whip, but Number Three only had a partial canister of pepper spray. Number One got down on the ground and started belly crawling toward the shack. He had more weapons, and he had the element of surprise on his side. He was going to win. I would have put money on it.

Someone walked up to the hooded man strapped to the chair. It was someone I hadn't seen before. He was wearing a black T-shirt and tight leather pants. The camera cut to a close-up of his hand. He was holding a shiny silver scalpel. The camera cut to a two-shot as Leather Pants made a short incision along the back of Hooded Man's left arm.

"Fuck you," Hooded Man shouted. He was hoarse, and his voice was muffled and distorted because of the hood. "Fuck you, and fuck your mother, you worthless piece of shit."

Leather Pants laughed. "You'll be begging for mercy before I'm done with you. I can promise you that. Just tell me what I want to know and I'll make it quick and painless."

"Fuck you."

Leather Pants made another incision, this time on the back of Hooded Man's right arm. Blood flowed from both wounds in a steady stream. Leather Pants grabbed a bottle of rubbing alcohol, screwed the top off, and doused the incisions.

Hooded Man screamed.

Number Three walked out to his porch, holding what looked like a pillowcase full of stones. He'd made his own weapon with the materials on hand. He'd been in a good position to go far in the game with the stun baton, but he didn't have it anymore. I'd stolen it from him. Now he had a bag of rocks. He spotted Number One crawling toward his house. You could see it in his eyes. Then, Number One saw that he'd been spotted. You could see it in *his* eyes. Number One rose and ran toward the house with the bullwhip in one hand and the nightstick in the other.

"You motherfucker," Hooded Man shouted. "Oh my god, you're going to fucking die."

"You really need to watch your mouth," Leather Pants said.

Leather Pants knelt down in front of the chair.

"What are you doing?" Hooded Man said. "Wait. Don't do that. Wait! Wait!"

The camera zoomed in to a close-up of Leather Pants pulling the skin of Hooded Man's scrotum taut with his left hand. With his right hand he made a midline incision with the scalpel. Blood oozed from the site.

Number Three stood there and let Number One come. When Number One got close enough, Number Three aimed the Mace canister toward him and started spraying. But Number One had been expecting it. He shielded his eyes with his arm, reared back, and cracked the whip. The canister flew from Number Three's hand and rattled to the back of the porch. Now Number One went at it with no mercy, lashing Number Three with the whip again and again and again. Number Three slung the bag of rocks toward Number One's head, but Number One ducked, and the bag dropped harmlessly to the ground. Now Number Three was weaponless. He retreated into his house, and Number One followed.

Hooded Man screamed and thrashed, but he was strapped to the wooden armchair with duct tape and the chair was bolted to the floor. He was helpless. Leather Pants reached into the bloody pouch with his ungloved fingers and with a cut here and a cut there liberated both of Hooded Man's testicles.

"There," Leather Pants said. "Now you won't have to worry about getting some bitch pregnant."

Hooded Man was heaving and gasping and screaming. I couldn't see the expression on his face, but I knew it was one of unimaginable terror.

"Fuck you, you cock-sucking son of a bitch," Hooded Man said.

Leather Pants rolled the testicles in his hand like a pair of dice and then threw them overhand at the wall behind Hooded Man. They splattered under the samurai sword. Leather Pants reached between Hooded Man's legs, grabbed his penis and stretched it out, and severed it at the base with the scalpel. He forced the organ into Hooded Man's mouth.

"Now who's the cocksucker?" Leather Pants said. He laughed big and loud.

I couldn't take it anymore.

"How much of this shit am I going to have to watch?" I shouted. "You hear me, Charles? Freeze? You sick motherfuckers."

"It's almost over," Charles said. "Keep watching. There's a nice twist at the end."

I looked at the screen. My stomach lurched, and I tasted the sour blackberries in the back of my throat. Number One discarded the whip and followed Number Three into the house with the nightstick raised overhead. He was moving in for the kill. That's what he thought. But when he got inside, there was a surprise waiting for him. Number Three had taken the mattress off his bed frame, as I had, but Number Three wasn't using his for a cooking surface. He had created an electrocution device.

The camera showed some flashback close-ups in quick succession, illustrating the method behind Number Three's madness. He had pulled the electrical cord from his lamp, stripped the ends to expose the wires, and wrapped the bare wires into the springs on his cot. The plug was on the floor, not yet inserted into the 120-volt outlet.

Number One looked around, puzzled. By the time he realized what was going on, it was too late.

Number Three had been standing behind the door. He jumped out, shoved Number One onto the bed frame, quickly grabbed the plug, and jammed it into the electrical outlet. There was a loud buzzing sound and Number One went into convulsions and started foaming at the mouth. He flopped around like a fish out of water, and blood oozed from his ears and eyeballs, and after a few seconds his scalp started smoking. He was being cooked from the inside.

Satisfied that Number One was good and dead, Number Three pulled the plug.

That scene between Number One and Number Three was the *nice twist at the end*, I thought.

But I was wrong.

The screen switched back to the drama in the garage interior, with Leather Pants and Hooded Man, and I gazed in horror as my life changed forever.

Leather Pants snatched the hood off the man strapped to the chair.

It was Joe Crawford, my best friend in the whole world.

Chapter Twenty-Nine

"No!" I shouted. "Oh, hell fucking no, you crazy motherfuckers."

I got up and kicked the television. I kicked it like I was punting a football, but the screen didn't break. It didn't go black. The video kept rolling. My heart bounced around in my chest like a bat in a can. I couldn't catch my breath.

Leather Pants grabbed the sword from the wall. He gripped it with both hands, like a baseball bat. I figured Joe's head was going to get chopped off now, the way Nathan Broadway's had. At least it was going to be over soon for my dear friend, I thought.

But I thought wrong.

Leather Pants dribbled some rubbing alcohol on all of Joe's wounds. He dribbled some on the incisions on the backs of Joe's arms and on his missing genitals. Joe had been on the verge of passing out, but the stinging alcohol woke him up. It brought him back to a high state of arousal. He snapped right out of it. His muscles tensed and he started screaming wildly.

Leather Pants capped the alcohol bottle and set it on the floor. He hefted the sword overhead like an axe, came down hard, and sliced Joe's left hand off at the wrist. The hand fell to the floor, and blood pulsed out in squirts from the severed artery in Joe's arm. That was it, I thought. Joe would bleed out quickly, and it would be over for him. But Leather Pants had other ideas. He walked off camera for a second and came back holding a metal clamp, the kind used on cars for radiator hoses. He fitted the clamp around Joe's arm, just above where his wrist used to be, and tightened it with a screwdriver. The bleeding stopped immediately. Leather Pants walked offstage again and this time came back holding an electric power drill. He pulled the trigger a couple of times, and the camera zoomed in on the rotating steel bit. God only knew what the crazy son of a bitch was going to do with that drill, but I refused to watch anymore. I walked outside to the porch and leaned over the railing and retched into the dirt.

"I'm going to kill you, Freeze. You hear me, you motherfucker? As long as I'm able to take a breath, my sole purpose in life is going to be to see you suffer and die."

Freeze came on the G-29. He laughed. "Good luck with that," he said. "You brought this on, you know. You're responsible for what's happening to your friend right now."

"Fuck you."

"No, it's true. You guessed he was going to be the ninth player, and you were right. You took all the fun out of it. You ruined my surprise. Now I'll have to find someone else, and there's not a lot of time left. If you had kept your mouth shut, your friend would be just fine right now. Let that be a lesson."

A mixture of guilt and anger roiled through me, as though my heart had been plucked from my chest and stuffed into an electric blender.

"Fuck you," I said again. "I *will* take your ass down, Freeze. Somehow I'm going to take your ass down."

He laughed again. "Since you won't stay in the house and watch, I'm going to give you a play-by-play commentary over the G-29. How about that? Javier Lorenzo, my beautiful young man in the leather pants, is now drilling a series of holes into the back of Mr. Crawford's skull. Javier is so good with tools. He's such a manly man. The bit must be getting pretty hot, because there's little plumes of smoke coming from the site where Javier is drilling. But it must not hurt much. Mr. Crawford isn't thrashing about and screaming like he was before. Oh, my. I hope he hasn't lost consciousness. That wouldn't be any fun, now would it? I'll be right back, Number Eight. I need to have a word with Javier."

I walked out to my fire pit. The squirrel looked done. The meat had turned from pink to golden brown. The embers had mostly died, so there was no chance of the animal burning now. Not that I cared. I didn't give a rat's ass about the squirrel now, or anything else. My best friend since sixth grade was dying a slow and horribly painful death, and there was nothing I could do about it. I couldn't help him, the way he'd helped me against Kenny and Calvin in the boys' restroom at Hallows Cove Elementary. And Freeze was right. It was my fault. I never should have let them know what I suspected, that Joe was going to be the ninth player. If I'd kept my mouth shut, Joe would still be OK. He would still have his balls and his dick and his left hand. He wouldn't be duct taped to a chair right now, with a lunatic in leather pants named Javier drilling holes in his head.

I wanted to run away. I wanted to yank the G-29 off my ear and fling it into the ashes and run and run and run until I was far away from this hell. I wanted to run away, but that would have been tantamount to suicide. If I ran, Freeze would push the red button on his remote and fry my heart with the internal defibrillator. I didn't want that to happen because now, more than ever, I wanted to stay alive. I wanted to stay alive and win the game and figure out a way to mercilessly obliterate Fatboy Billionaire. I wanted to shove him into a giant meat grinder and make hamburger out of his fat ass and then feed him to his mysterious Sexy

Bastards. I didn't want there to be any evidence that he had ever existed.

But I needed to win the game first. I was determined to win the game.

Freeze came back over the G-29. "Hello, Number Eight."

"Fuck you."

"My, my. You're so impolite, Number Eight. We do need to teach you some manners. Anyway, I just wanted to let you know that your friend Joe Crawford has expired. A shame. I expected to have much more fun with him. Javier should have been more careful. Javier deserves a good old-fashioned spanking, don't you think?"

"I think he deserves a lot more than that," I said. "How about you let me deliver his punishment?"

Silence, and then, "Well now, I hadn't considered that. But it might actually be something to think about. I'll get back to you, Number Eight. Interesting idea."

And with that he was gone.

Chapter Thirty

Joe Crawford had been more than a friend to me. I didn't feel like a whole person anymore. I felt as though a piece of my own flesh had been ripped away and tossed into a wood chipper. I sat on the porch and grieved until there was nothing left.

Depleted, hollow, but determined more than ever now to find a way to win, I spent some time trying to think of strategies to eliminate the four remaining players. I figured I would start with Number Three tomorrow. I knew where he lived, and I knew about the trap he'd set for Number One. And he didn't have any weapons. Taking him out would be a piece of cake, I thought. Maybe not a piece of cake, but pretty fucking easy.

It troubled me some that I was devising ways to kill innocent men. None of them had done anything wrong. They certainly hadn't done anything to me. They'd been unlucky, that was all. They'd been chosen to play Snuff Tag 9, and now they were going to die at the hands of a rock star turned private investigator turned security consultant. Freeze had me right where he wanted me. He'd turned me into a malicious killer.

I walked over to the fire pit and lifted the squirrel from my makeshift grill. The fire had died and the meat was cool to the touch. I tore one of the hind legs off, walked back to the porch, and started gnawing on it. The flesh was tough and still a little pink next to the bone. It had a wild and gamey flavor. Could have used some salt and pepper and Tabasco sauce and a side of biscuits and gravy.

I should have been starving, but I wasn't. I really didn't even feel like eating, but I knew I needed to keep my strength up. One way or another I was going to win this game. One way or another I was going to avenge Joe's brutal murder. I was going to kill Number Three and Number Four and Number Six and Number Seven. Come to think of it, I probably wouldn't have to kill them all. Some of them would probably kill each other. At any rate, I was going to see that every one of them was eliminated.

And Number Nine. I wondered who it would be now. I had an idea, but I certainly wasn't going to say anything this time. Didn't want to jinx it. I had an idea it was going to be Javier Lorenzo. Leather Pants. I wanted it to be him. I'd planted the notion in Freeze's mind, and I'd heard the enthusiasm in his voice. It would make a great finale for his reality show. Me against the guy who'd killed my best friend. Heavy drama. Freeze couldn't have scripted it any better if he'd tried.

I sat on the porch and ate the whole squirrel and then tossed the bones into the dirt. I still had the rest of the day off from the game, and I needed to spend the time wisely. I needed to get more food. I fingered through the boiled organs and entrails in the skillet, picked out what I figured was the liver, and sliced it into two pieces. I nibbled a tiny corner off one of the pieces. It was liver. It tasted awful. I figured the catfish would eat it up.

I grabbed my fishing rig and headed for the pond. I still had my stun baton and the nunchucks in my pockets, and the survival knife was in its sheath on my belt. I didn't anticipate needing any of the weapons, but I felt better having them. Sort of a security blanket. A *false* security blanket, if I wanted to be honest with myself. And really there was nothing stopping another player from coming by and stealing everything while I wasn't home. So I took the weapons with me.

I made it to the pond and cast my baited hook into the water. I got a hit almost immediately. Something big. I pulled it in slowly, thinking the line was surely going to break, but it didn't. The line held and I landed the catch on the bank. It wasn't a catfish. It was a snapping turtle. As big around as a salad bowl. The bent nail was hooked through the back of its jaw on the left side. It was a powerful animal, and it was angry as hell. I wasn't about to put my fingers anywhere near its mouth to remove the hook. It was fierce and furious and its jaw was made for clamping down on things and not letting go. I carefully picked it up by the tail and held it at arm's length, away from my body. I didn't know what to do with it. It probably weighed ten pounds or more. It represented quite a bit of food, but it was going to be trouble to deal with. I knew there were people who ate turtles, but I'd never cleaned and cooked one myself. I didn't know how to handle it. I thought about letting it go, but I knew it would die anyway now with the nail in its jaw. I decided I would keep it and try to eat it. I cut the line with my knife a few feet from the end and tied it to a cypress stump near the water. The snapper could stay moist there, but it was on a short leash. It couldn't go anywhere. It tried. It struggled to get away, but it couldn't.

I tied my other hook to the line and baited it with the other piece of liver. I walked thirty feet or so and cast into a different spot. I didn't want any more turtles. I wanted a catfish. I waited about fifteen minutes and then sat on the bank and waited some more. No bites. I sat in the same spot for over an hour without a hit. That's the way it is with fishing. Sometimes you can go all day without a nibble. Other times you get lucky and they swallow the hook as soon as it hits the water. Today was not a lucky day. I pulled the line in and wrapped it around the pole. Untied the turtle and picked it up by the tail again and headed home.

On the way, the alarm sounded for play to resume. I ignored it. It didn't affect me. I had the day off.

When I got to the house I went ahead and dealt with the turtle first thing. I used some dental floss to hang it by its tail from a tree branch, and then I cut its head off with my knife. It was a sorrowful thing to watch, because it didn't die right away. Its legs moved for several long minutes while the blood drained from its neck. Like it was trying to run to safety. It finally died and hung there limp while the last of its blood dripped to the ground. I felt sorry that I'd killed it. It had clung to life so fiercely. It seemed to have been pleading for mercy right before I sawed through its tough, gristly neck. I could have granted it a pardon. I could have wrestled the nail from its jaw and set it free back at the pond, where it would have lived happily ever after. Of course it hadn't been pleading for mercy. I was attributing human emotions to another species. There's a word for that, but I couldn't think of it. I was attributing human emotions to an animal with a brain the size of a pea. It didn't think. It didn't have feelings. All it had was an instinct to survive. Its sole purpose in life was to eat and make baby turtles. I was higher on the food chain than it was. That's the way it worked. Something had to die so I could live. Today it was the turtle. Tomorrow it would be something else. That's the way it worked.

But I still felt bad about it.

For some reason I felt worse about slaughtering that goddamn snapping turtle than I did about the human being I'd killed yesterday. Number Five. The architect from Bainbridge, Georgia. The marathon runner. But with Number Five, it was eventually going to come down to me or him. That wasn't the case with the turtle. I wished I hadn't killed it, but I had. I had killed it, and there was nothing I could do now to take it back.

I wondered if I was losing my mind.

I shouted at the sky. "Fuck it," I said.

"Hello, Number Eight."

It was Charles on the G-29.

"Fuck it," I said.

"Fuck it?"

"Yeah. Fuck it."

"OK. Well, I just wanted to let you know there's going to be a battle soon. Should be a good one. I want you to walk inside so you can see it on your monitor."

"I've seen enough for one day. Don't you think?"

"Sorry, but it's mandatory viewing. Go inside the house now, Number Eight. Freeze's orders."

"Fuck it," I said.

But I followed the orders. I went inside. Sat on my mattress and looked at the screen. It was blank. The show hadn't started yet. I sat there and looked at my own reflection. My cheeks looked sunken and haggard. Bruised and scabbed and unshaven. I pulled my shirt up. My ribs were showing. I'd lost weight. Maybe ten pounds since the last genuine meal I'd eaten. If I made it out of the swamp alive, maybe I would market the experience as a weight loss program. The Snuff Tag 9 Diet. Slim and trim in just five days! Five days of starving in the wilderness with eight people determined to kill you and an insane demigod orchestrating everything and watching from afar. It would be a huge success. I would make millions.

I looked at the screen and shook my head. I looked like shit. Another battle was coming on, Charles had said. Another player was going to die, and I didn't give a damn. I was happy about it. One less for me to kill. I didn't want to watch, but I was numb to it now. After seeing what they'd done to Joe, I was desensitized to any other horrors they could conjure up.

It had been over ten minutes since I'd walked into the house and sat on my mattress, and the screen was still blank. For some reason I started thinking about what The Potato Man had said in my dream. *The change on the aloe fence.* Maybe it meant something, but I couldn't figure it out. Maybe it meant something, or maybe it was just some nonsense manufactured by my subconscious. It felt like some sort of profound knowledge was just beyond my grasp, but my rational mind told me that was probably not the case. It was probably just bullshit. *The change on the aloe fence.* I was still thinking about it when the flat screen buzzed to life.

There was an aerial shot of an open field. One player was chasing another. I could see the red jerseys, but not the numbers on them. The camera was too far away. They must have been tracking the players with a helicopter. The gap was narrowing. The chaser was gaining ground on the one being chased. It reminded me of *National Geographic* footage. A lion running after a zebra or something. The camera zoomed in closer. Now I could see the numbers. Number Seven was chasing Number Four. Number Four was the electrical engineer from Indianapolis. The gym rat. Five nine, one seventy, tested positive for steroids. Freeze said he was aggressive and unpredictable, but right now he was running like a scared bunny. Number Seven was the diving instructor from Palatka, Florida. The former Navy SEAL. Five ten, one sixty. Freeze said he knew a hundred ways to kill a man with his bare hands, and I had a feeling I was fixing to witness one of them.

Number Seven was gaining on Number Four, slowly but surely. Both of the men were obviously in top physical condition, but Number Seven was a little faster. A little swifter on his feet. As the gap narrowed, the camera zoomed in even closer. Then the video cut to a point-of-view shot, from the front camera on

Number Seven's collar. I could hear Number Seven's rhythmic huffing as he ran at top speed, and I could see the back of Number Four's jersey. Number Four zigzagged, trying to avoid capture, but it was no use. Number Seven tackled him to the ground. For a minute I wondered why neither of them was brandishing weapons, and then I remembered that the alarm to resume the game had sounded but not the alarm for weapons. This battle was going to be hand-to-hand, mano a mano. Like a UFC cage fight, only there was no referee and only one man would walk away alive.

Number Four and Number Seven wrestled around in the sandy scrub grass for a few seconds, and then Number Four actually ended up on top. It surprised me. I thought Number Seven, the Navy SEAL, would dispose of his opponent in quick order, but so far Number Four was holding his own. He was doing more than holding his own. He was winning. He straddled Number Seven's chest and pummeled his face with closed fists. All those hours in the gym were paying off. Even with his clothes on, you could tell Number Four was built like a brick shithouse. He was all sloped shoulders and broad chest and biceps like tree trunks. He kept beating Number Seven mercilessly. He was beating him to a pulp. Blood gushed from Number Seven's nose, and when he opened his mouth I could see that some of his front teeth had been knocked out. How he remained conscious I didn't know, but he did. He not only remained conscious, he started rallying. He bucked and grabbed Number Four by the throat and squeezed with all his might until Number Four was forced to roll away to break the hold.

Multiple cameras showed the scene from a variety of angles as the two men stood and faced each other, circled each other, hands at the ready. They did their little dance for a while, each looking for one small opening that might lead to an advantage.

Number Four had drawn first blood, but now it was Number Seven's turn to shine. With lightning speed, seeming to defy gravity, he jumped up and kicked Number Four in the face with the heel of his boot. He'd obviously had some martial arts training. Probably tae kwon do. At least a first-degree black belt, I guessed. After the kick he came down hard on the bridge of Number Four's nose with his right elbow. There was a loud crunch, the sound of bone shattering. It was a devastating blow. Number Four staggered backward, covered his face with his hands in an effort to prevent further assault, but Number Seven was like a predatory cat now moving in for the kill. He kicked Number Four's left knee, kicked it so hard it bent backward. It was painful to watch and even more painful to hear. The sight of the joint being wrenched in the wrong direction was accompanied by the sickening sound of ligaments and tendons being torn apart, followed immediately by a series of agonizing guttural yawps from somewhere deep in Number Four's massive chest. He fell. He was done. His leg was destroyed. There was no way he was getting back up. Number Seven started kicking him in the ribs. More bone crunching. All he had to do was fall on Number Four's throat with one knee, but Number Seven seemed intent on inflicting as much pain as possible before delivering the fatal blow. The game had turned him into something not quite human. Even with all his physical and mental training as a SEAL, Freeze's idea of a sport had turned Number Seven into a monster.

But Number Four wasn't quite finished yet. He reached down and grabbed something from one of his flap pockets on his pants. The camera zoomed in. It was the stun baton. Number Four pulled the trigger and delivered an eight-hundred-thousand-volt arc of electricity to the leg Number Seven was kicking him with. Number Seven went stiff and then fell to the ground.

It seemed the tables had turned again.

Number Four writhed in agony. He had a lot of injuries. The most severe were the crushed nose and the ruined knee and the broken ribs. They were severe, but not life-threatening.

All the king's horses and all the king's men could have put Number Four back together again. A good team of surgeons and a few months of convalescence and Number Four would be back in business, back in the gym doing squats and presses and curls eight hours a day and drinking protein shakes. He scooted toward Number Seven with his elbows. Grunting. Moaning. Every millimeter a gut-wrenching mile.

Number Seven was on his back and completely unconscious. The high-voltage stun gun had knocked him out cold. But had I missed something? Had the alarm for weapons sounded? It must have. I never heard it, but it must have gone off. Otherwise Number Four would have been terminated immediately. That was the rule. If you used a weapon during a period when weapons weren't allowed, your defibrillator would discharge and your heart would stop beating. No questions asked. Number Four was still alive, so the alarm for weapons must have sounded. It must have sounded without me hearing it. That was the only plausible explanation.

Number Four inched closer and closer to where Number Seven lay on the ground. There was a momentary dissolve, and then the camera showed a close-up of Number Four's right hand. He'd tossed the stun baton and replaced it with his second weapon, a set of brass knuckles. All he needed to do was get in the right position and he could easily bash Number Seven's head in. He grunted and scooted and moaned and heaved, and he was about two feet from certain victory when Number Seven started to stir.

"Motherfucker," Number Seven said. He opened his eyes and the camera switched to his point of view. Number Four's brass-wrapped fist was above him and coming down fast. Number Seven rolled right, and Number Four's fist slammed into the sand.

Number Four was practically helpless now. He had the brass knuckles, but he couldn't get up. His knee was shredded. He turned on his back and said, "Please, I don't want to die."

Number Seven stood. Wobbly. Breathing hard. He didn't say anything. He was a SEAL. A professional killer. Professional killers don't usually say anything. They just kill you. He staggered over and stomped Number Four's face with his boot. He stomped it again and again and again, until Number Four's skull crumbled like a walnut shell.

"Nobody wants to die," Number Seven said. "But today it was your turn, bitch."

The camera moved to a close-up of Number Seven's face. A voice from offstage said, "What does it feel like to stomp a man's skull in like that?"

It was Freeze. I recognized the voice.

Number Seven was still breathing hard. "It doesn't feel like anything. What do you mean?"

"Do you feel any remorse?"

"Hell no. It was me or him. And when did the fucking alarm for weapons sound? I could have put him away a lot faster if I'd been able to use my knife and chucks."

So Number Seven had gotten the same weapons as me. The survival knife and the nunchucks. Quite a coincidence. But I had a third weapon now. I had the stun baton. Now that I'd seen it in action, how powerful it was, I was even more pleased that I'd taken the risk to steal it from Number Three.

"We were a split second away from zapping his heart with the defibrillator," Freeze said, responding to Number Seven's inquiry about the weapons alarm.

"When were you going to do it? After he broke my face with those brass knuckles?"

The screen faded to black.

Chapter Thirty-One

The alarm sounded for play to cease. I figured that was it for the day.

Number Four was dead, which meant the game was down to me and three other players: Number Three, the radiologist from Quincy, Illinois, the six-foot-five-inch giant I'd stolen the stun gun from; Number Six, the ex-marine airline pilot with the high IQ; and Number Seven, the former Navy SEAL who'd just stomped the fuck out of Number Four.

Number Three was weaponless. He'd used all his pepper spray, and I had taken his stun baton. Number Seven had a survival knife and a pair of nunchucks, the same weapons I'd picked from the cart the night before the game started. Number Six I didn't know about. He was the only player I hadn't seen yet. Number Six was a wild card.

I wondered if the other players had seen me on video at some point. I wondered if they were sizing me up, analyzing my situation the way I was theirs. Probably so. There was no reason to believe they weren't. Thinking about it sort of eroded any illusion I had of an edge.

Tomorrow was day three. I figured Freeze would stage two
battles—me against one of the remaining players and the other
two against each other. I'd wanted to go after Number Three, and
with a little luck maybe Freeze would let it play out that way. Me
against Number Three, and Number Six against Number Seven.
I would probably win against Number Three, and Number Seven
would probably win against Number Six. That would leave me
and Number Seven to face each other on day four. Then the vic-
tor of that battle would face Number Nine in the finale on day
five. That's the way I figured it might go down, but it was just a
guess. It would go down the way Freeze wanted it to go down. He
had the power to capriciously manipulate the game to his heart's
content, and there wasn't much I or the other players could do
about it.

Something suddenly occurred to me. Number Nine was
probably not one person waiting in the wings. Number Nine was
probably going to be chosen from a pool of players, depending
on which of the initial eight made it to the finale. If I made it
to the finale, for example, it would have made sense for Number
Nine to be Joe Crawford. And now that Joe was dead, it would
make sense for me to face his killer. Javier Lorenzo. Leather Pants.
On an emotional level, for everyone involved and for whatever
depraved audience these videos were distributed to, it made sense
for me to square off against Leather Pants. But if Number Seven
made it to the finale, it would make more dramatic sense for him
to face a player that meant something to *him*. That was my theory.
Number Nine was going to be chosen based on who made it to
the final battle.

I had a feeling it would be me and Leather Pants in the final
battle. I had a feeling Freeze would rig it to go that way. That
would be the ultimate dramatic conclusion. Me against the man
who mutilated Joe Crawford. Me against the lowlife motherfucker
who had butchered my best friend.

I walked out to the tree where I'd hung the snapping turtle. The blood had stopped dripping and the legs had stopped moving. The turtle was completely drained and completely dead. I cut the double strand of dental floss with my knife and the animal fell and landed in the sand with a thud. I carried it to the porch and picked up the skillet. I thought about trying to save the squirrel guts for fish bait, but they had started to smell bad already and it was too late to go fishing anyway so I tossed them into the ashes in the fire pit. I took the turtle inside and washed it off and lowered it upside down into the skillet and filled the skillet with water.

I set the skillet on the porch with the turtle in it and went out to gather some firewood. It was starting to get dark. The purple glow of sunset saturated the landscape. I hurried and made several trips and piled enough branches next to my pit to keep the fire going for a long time. I'd never cooked a turtle before, but I figured it would take quite a while to boil the shell off. Just seemed like it would. I didn't want to go back in the woods after dark if I could avoid it. I had the flashlight, but I still hadn't been given any replacement batteries. Freeze said I would have to earn them. I wondered what that would entail.

I broke some branches into three-foot sections, put some twigs and dry leaves under them, and started the fire with the butane lighter. I'd used the lighter three times. According to Freeze, I had six more flicks of my Bic before the fuel ran dry. Plenty, I thought. Even if I made it to the finale, I would only be out here three more days. Two fires per day. Plenty.

When the fire got going good, I rested the skillet over it on the bedsprings and stood there and watched. The stainless steel skillet got hot right away, and amazingly the turtle's legs started moving again. The poor son of a bitch still wasn't dead yet. The decapitation wound must have clotted off. There must have still been enough blood circulating to keep him going. And going.

And going. He was like the goddamn Energizer Bunny. Now he was going to be cooked alive in his own shell. I felt like the biggest asshole in the world. I felt very sorry for the turtle. I felt sorry for him until the steam started rising from the skillet. The wonderful aroma of the meat boiling reminded me of my hunger. As pitiful as the creature seemed, and as cruel as my deeds seemed, the turtle's death would not be in vain. The turtle would not go to waste. He would live on inside me, and I would live to see Freeze strung up by his balls.

"Hello, Number Eight."

Speak of the devil.

"What is it now, Freeze?"

It had been a long day, and I was getting annoyed. I just wanted to be left alone. I wanted to cook my turtle and eat it and go to bed.

"You sound a little irritable," Freeze said. "What's wrong? You didn't enjoy your day off?"

"I was forced to watch the best friend I've ever known have his cock sliced off and shoved in his mouth. What do you think?"

I wanted to kill that bastard Freeze more than anything in the world.

"I think the night is still young," he said. "Go inside. I have one more thing to show you."

There was no point in arguing. I took the skillet off the fire and set it on the porch. I didn't want it to boil dry and ruin the turtle. That would have been inexcusable. I walked inside, switched on the lamp, washed my hands and face at the sink.

I sat on the mattress, and a few seconds later the television monitor blinked on. The screen was black except for the game's simple logo: SNUFF TAG 9 in bold white letters. The name said it all.

"All the remaining players are in their houses now," Freeze said. "And all are watching this broadcast live as I speak. I trust you can all hear me. Hello, everyone."

There was a brief pause, and then Freeze continued: "Congratulations, Number Three, Number Six, Number Seven, and Number Eight. All of you have made it to day three. Hump day, if you will. We've seen a lot of great action on day one and day two, and we got a lot of great footage. You all did an excellent job, and I thank you for that. Unfortunately, two more of you must die tomorrow. I will contact you individually to let you know who you'll be fighting and where to go. That will be in the morning. But tonight, I have a nice surprise for you. Tonight, I'm going to introduce player Number Nine. I'm going to introduce him, but let me make it clear that he will not be participating in tomorrow's battles. He will not enter the game until day four. At that time, Snuff Tag Nine will be down to three players: the two who win their battles tomorrow and Number Nine. Some of you might have heard some rumors, and some of you might think you have everything figured out. You might think the game is rigged, that I choose who survives and who dies based on the players I think would make the best match for the finale. You might even think Number Nine is chosen for that reason, for the sake of the best possible dramatic conclusion. Let me assure you that is not the case. None of this is scripted. Number Nine will be put in the game on day four, so he might or might not even make it to the finale. The game is not rigged. Each and every one of you has the equal opportunity to win the game and live in luxury for the rest of your life.

"And here's another thing. I've learned through the years that the winner is not always the physically strongest of the bunch. In fact, that's rarely the case. What happened to Number Four today is a prime example. He had a history of going to the gym six days a week. He had a body like Conan the Barbarian. Yet he lost. Congratulations to Number Seven, by the way. In all the years I've been producing Snuff Tag Nine, that was one of the finest battles I've ever had the pleasure to have witnessed. But no, it's usually not one of the big muscular guys who wins. It's usually someone with great endurance and great mental fortitude. High powers of concentration. That's why I choose players with a variety of backgrounds, players from vastly different walks of life. Throwing a bunch of stupid gladiators in a ring would seem boring to me. It's much more interesting when someone wins through wit and cunning rather than brute strength. I remember one time, three years ago I think, when…"

Freeze was rambling on and on and on, and it was driving me nuts. I was tired and hungry and desperately in need of some downtime.

I interrupted him in midsentence. "Get on with it, Freeze," I said. "Are you going to show us Number Nine or not? I'm sure he wants to eat and get to bed as much as the rest of us."

There was a long pause. "Did I say *he*?" Freeze said. "Whoops. My mistake."

The Snuff Tag 9 logo dissolved and a face slowly faded in on top of it.

A face very familiar to me.

Number Nine wasn't Leather Pants, and it wasn't someone who meant something to one of the other players.

Number Nine was my wife.

Number Nine was Juliet.

Chapter Thirty-Two

I tried to stand, but my legs wouldn't cooperate. They buckled and I fell to my knees.

I fell to my knees and covered my face with my hands and wept. I lost it. I cried like a baby.

This couldn't be happening.

I thought nothing could surprise me after what I'd seen happen to Joe Crawford. I thought nothing could shock me, but I was wrong. Seeing Juliet's face appear on that television screen was like…it was like nothing I could think of. There were no words to describe my thoughts and feelings at that moment. I broke down. I couldn't take it anymore.

I shouted hysterically: "I swear to God, Freeze, if she's harmed in any way—"

"What will you do?" he said. "Nothing, that's what. You can only do what I allow you to do. That's the deal, Number Eight, even if you win the game. That's the deal for the rest of your life. Now listen up, gentlemen. The woman you see on your monitor is Number Nine. If you make it through to day four, you'll definitely be seeing her again. She's a player, just like the rest of you. Don't treat her any differently because she's a woman. She's smart and she has weapons and she will kill you in a heartbeat. She wants to survive every bit as much as the rest of you. OK? Treat her the same as any other player. Treat her with the same respect and fear you would a man. That's all for tonight. I will talk to you all in the morning. Good night and pleasant dreams."

My heart sank. Freeze was right. There was nothing I could do.

Only one person could win the game. Only one person could walk away alive. Either Juliet would have to die or I would have to die. Or we would both have to die. That was always a possibility. But both of us living was not a possibility. At least one of us was going to die on day four or day five. That's the way it was, and there was nothing we could do to change it.

I decided then and there that if it came down to Juliet and me in the finale, I would commit suicide. I would fall on my knife and end it so she could live. As much as I wanted to exact revenge on Freeze, there was no way I could kill my wife. I loved her too much. I loved her more than I loved myself.

The fact that we'd been separated for a long time didn't matter. She was my soul mate, and I knew it was only a matter of time before we got back together.

Juliet's heart had been broken when she found out I'd slept with another woman in Los Angeles. I slept with another woman, it happened, but I had been drugged and brainwashed by the leader of a white supremacist cult called the Harvest Angels. I didn't even know my own name at the time. I had no recollection of my past, no memory of being married.

I knew in time Juliet would get over it and take me back.

But now there was no time. In two days, one of us would be dead.

I felt ill. Nauseated. I had no interest in food anymore. I walked out to the porch and lifted the turtle from the skillet and heaved it like a shot put into the darkness. Fuck that turtle. The fire ants could feast on it. I no longer had any feelings about it. I no longer had any feelings about anything. Life was over for me. I was defeated.

I went inside and gulped some water from the faucet and turned the lamp off and collapsed on my mattress. It was a little after ten o'clock. I lay there on my back with my eyes open and stared at the blackness. I was exhausted, but I knew I would never be able to sleep. I didn't care. It didn't matter. Nothing mattered.

I thought about everything I'd been through since this ordeal started. I should have taken that letter more seriously, the letter Nathan Broadway received from The Sexy Bastards. I never should have assumed it was just a ruse to get him out of the house for the evening. A death threat is a death threat. I should have insisted he take it to the police. Maybe he would still be alive now if I had. Instead, he was tortured and decapitated and his head was slung at my windshield. In my mind I could still see the smear it left when it bounced off. Nathan Broadway was dead, and it was my fault. *Epic fail*, as my daughter, Brittney, would say. That was the fatal error, the one that led to everything else in this fucked-up scenario. My abduction. Joe's murder. And now Juliet. All because of one rich, fat son of a bitch's obsession with a video game.

But why me? Why did Nathan Broadway call me in the first place? He said I was third in the phone book. Why couldn't PI number one or PI number two meet him somewhere on a Sunday to discuss his problem? It's not like private investigators keep bankers' hours. You meet when it's convenient for your client. If it's a Sunday, it's a Sunday. That's how you make your living, by being available all day every day. If PI number one or PI number two had met him that Sunday, it would be one of them lying on this thin mattress out in the middle of nowhere shivering now and thinking about all this shit. So why me?

Because. That's why. Because I'm an unlucky person. Because sometimes I take jobs that nobody else wants. Because I'm a loser. Just fucking because.

I was lying there feeling sorry for myself and wondering how everything could have possibly gotten so fucked up when, somehow, I fell asleep. It was like someone hit a switch. I fell asleep and immediately went spinning into the strangest dream I'd ever had in my life.

Joe Crawford was in my dream, but he was wearing blue coveralls and a red ball cap and his face kept changing. It kept changing to the guy I saw in the woods messing with one of the cameras, the guy I thought I recognized but couldn't remember from where. Joe and I were adults in the dream, but suddenly we were back in sixth grade in the boys' restroom at Hallows Cove Elementary.

Kenny and Calvin had taken my milk money and forced me into one of the stalls and they had shoved my head into the toilet bowl. In my dream, just as it had been in real life, the bowl wasn't clean. It was full of Calvin's smelly urine, and they shoved my face right down into it. I thought those stupid pricks were going to drown me, and then a voice from outside the stall said, "Let him go."

Kenny and Calvin turned around. Through the water dripping from my forehead I saw Joe Crawford standing there outside the stall with his fists clenched. Only it wasn't Joe Crawford. His face had changed. It was the guy in blue coveralls and a red ball cap. The guy I knew I'd seen before but couldn't remember when or where.

"Get out of here, Crawford," Kenny said. He called him Crawford, although in my dream it really wasn't Joe anymore. "This ain't none of your business."

"I'm making it my business," the guy wearing the blue coveralls and red ball cap said. "Now let him go before I kick your ass."

Calvin bolted out of the stall, cocked his fist, and swung at Red Ball Cap's head, but Red Ball Cap ducked and punched Calvin in the stomach and pushed him into the urine trough.

"You're dead, Crawford," Kenny said. He went for Red Ball Cap, but I grabbed his foot and tripped him and he fell face-first into the stall's metal doorframe. I pushed him to the floor and straddled him and slugged his face repeatedly. The bell rang and Red Ball Cap and I walked out of the boys' restroom together.

"Who are you?" I asked.

"You can call me Red," he said.

"Do I know you?"

"You watched me die."

"I watched Joe die," I said. "You're not Joe."

"You watched me die," he said again.

As we walked an endless hallway lined with lockers on both sides, The Potato Man darted by and said, "The change on the aloe fence."

That ridiculous phrase again. *The change on the aloe fence.*

I looked at Red. "What does that mean?" I said.

"The chains on the elephants?" he said. "I think it's pretty obvious what it means."

The dream dissolved and I sat up straight in bed gasping for air. I shook it off and took a few deep breaths.

After my heart stopped racing, I smiled.

I smiled because now I knew.

Chapter Thirty-Three

I knew who he was, the guy in the blue coveralls and red ball cap. The guy I'd seen adjusting one of the cameras when I was squirrel hunting. He knew he had made a mistake, and he ran off when he noticed me. At the time, I tried to think when and where we'd met previously, but I couldn't remember.

Now I remembered. I finally remembered where I'd seen him before.

You watched me die, he'd said in my dream.

And I had.

I had seen him the night I was abducted, when I was still naked in the wire cage.

Freeze had shown me a video of a guy from a previous game, a guy wearing a number 6 jersey. He was outside, somewhere in the thick brush in the swamp, and it was daytime. He was walking along a row of trees connected by lengths of the red barrier tape that marked the boundaries of the playing field. He looked around, ducked under the tape, and ran into the woods on the other side. He sprinted twenty feet or so, stopped, and gasped and clutched his chest and fell to the ground and died.

That's what will happen if you try to escape, Freeze had said.

But Freeze was full of shit. The video was a fake. Oh, it was a great acting job. Had me fooled all the way. The guy wearing the red number 6 jersey could have won an Oscar. But I saw him in blue coveralls and a red ball cap weeks later, messing with a camera while I was hunting squirrels. He never really died.

Since the video was fake, maybe some other things were fake too.

When I was watching Number Four and Number Seven battle on the TV monitor, Number Four pulled his stun baton and used it during a period when weapons weren't allowed. He broke a cardinal rule, and punishment for that was supposed to be immediate termination. Freeze was supposed to push a button and activate the internal defibrillator and cook Number Four's heart like a piece of toast.

But it didn't happen.

Did Freeze let the game go on for drama's sake? Or did he simply not have the power to activate the defibrillators after all? And if he didn't have the power to activate the defibrillators, why go to all the trouble of having them surgically inserted in the first place?

The chains on the elephants.

After Joe Crawford and I became friends in sixth grade, his parents took us to the circus one Saturday night. They paid my way in and bought me peanuts and cotton candy and an orange soda. It was a hell of a nice thing for them to do. They knew my mother was dead. They knew my stepfather was a drunk and wouldn't fork over the money for me to go. So they paid my way, and that night at the circus became one of my fondest childhood memories. We got there early, and on our way to the big top we just happened to walk past the stalls where they housed the elephants.

"How do they keep them from running away?" I asked.

Mr. Crawford, Joe's dad, was a knowledgeable guy. He was like a walking encyclopedia. He seemed to have an answer for any question you asked.

"See the chains on the elephants' rear legs?" he said.

I nodded. "But the elephants are big and strong, strong enough to break loose from those chains. So why don't they?"

"They're big and strong enough now," Mr. Crawford said, "but they weren't when they were babies. That's when the trainers put the chains on their legs. When elephants are babies, they try to break loose but they can't. Eventually they realize it's futile. They give up. It's a psychological thing. They don't try to break loose from the chains because they think they can't."

I had a hunch the subdermal lump under my left collar bone wasn't really a defibrillator at all. I had a hunch it was just a useless hunk of metal, a dummy. It kept us under Freeze's thumb because we *thought* it could instantly kill us. It was a psychological thing, just like the chains on the elephants.

The more I thought about it, the more I was convinced. A remotely controlled killing device, like the defibrillator was supposed to be, didn't really even make much sense. With cell phones and satellite televisions and global positioning systems bouncing frequencies all over the planet twenty-four/sevens, it seemed like stray signals might accidentally set such a device off. *Whoops! There goes another player.* Freeze couldn't afford to let that happen. He needed the players to die in battle, not accidentally. He needed them to feed his sadistic cravings, his addiction to drama and blood and pain.

My heart wasn't going to be zapped if I tried to escape or if someone surgically removed the device. The defibrillator was a fake, just like the video I'd watched that first night at Freeze's house. That was my hunch. That was my theory, but I needed to test it somehow. If I crossed the boundary and my hypothesis was wrong, I wouldn't get a second chance. My heart would go into ventricular fibrillation and I would collapse and die.

I needed to verify my hunch, but I didn't want to die doing it. I needed a guinea pig. I needed to test my theory on another player, and the only player it made any sense to try to test it on was Number Three. I knew where he lived, and I knew he didn't have any weapons.

I knew where Number Three's house was, but it was going to be a problem navigating the woods and finding it at night.

I walked outside. It was overcast. No moon, no stars. Darker than dark. The only thing I could see were the embers glowing red from my fire pit. I thought about trying to make some kind of torch, but then I realized I needed to work under the cloak of darkness anyway. I needed to be invisible to the cameras between my house and Number Three's. If I was found roaming around at night, it wouldn't matter if the defibrillator was a fake or not. They would hunt me down and execute me.

I went inside and stuffed some things in my backpack. I looked at my watch. It was almost midnight. Six hours or so before sunrise. Six hours to do everything I needed to do, and I needed to do a lot of things. There was no time to waste, no time to formulate any sort of detailed plan. I would have to improvise as I went, play it ad lib.

Just the way I liked it.

Chapter Thirty-Four

I knew the general direction to Number Three's house, but I figured I would need to consult my compass at least a couple of times along the way. My only light source was the butane cigarette lighter, and according to Freeze, I only had enough fuel left for six more three-second ignitions.

But maybe I wouldn't need an actual flame.

I switched the lamp off, held the compass in my left hand and the lighter in my right. I flicked the flint wheel with my thumb, but I didn't depress the little gas pedal that opened the fuel valve. My idea worked. There was a spark, but no fire, and the spark provided enough light for me to see the compass for a brief second. Success.

I grabbed my backpack and headed out. I had my nunchucks in one pocket and the stun baton in another and my knife in its sheath. I carried the spear I'd made for squirrel hunting, using it the way a blind person uses a cane. It kept me from tripping over vines and from running into trees, and I figured it might come in handy as an extra weapon.

I crept through the woods as quietly as possible, knowing the cameras picked up audio as well as video. I probably wasn't making any more noise than a fox or a possum or a raccoon. Freeze, or whoever was keeping watch overnight, thought I was home in bed, and that's what they needed to keep thinking. Getting caught would mean certain death. An hour earlier I would have welcomed it, but not now. Now I had hope. I wanted to live, and I wanted Juliet to live, and I was going to do everything in my power to see that we did.

I flicked the flint wheel and looked at the compass and adjusted my course. If my calculations were correct, Number Three's house was only about a quarter mile from my current position. I walked on, hoping I didn't step in a hole and break a leg or run into a tree branch and poke out an eyeball.

Suddenly the woods ran out, and I knew I was in the clearing of Number Three's house. I got on my hands and knees and crawled through the dry grass. I couldn't actually see the shack, but I knew its approximate position from memory. I stayed low. I didn't want to be an easy target if a light came on.

I crawled until I felt the wooden planks on the porch. I was exhausted. Sweat was dripping from every pore. I took a few minutes to catch my breath and try to devise a plan of attack. I figured Number Three was asleep in bed. All was dark and quiet. You could have heard a mouse fart. I remembered the electrocution device he had constructed from his bed frame and lamp cord, so I didn't think it would be prudent to bust in through the front door. The device might be standing guard, and if so that would be it for me. Curtains. Crispy critters. The window was the only other way in, but you can't just dive through glass like they do in the movies. If you dive through glass like they do in the movies, you get cut to ribbons and bleed to death.

I could have broken the window with the butt of my knife and cleared the glass enough to crawl through safely, but that would have been noisy and it would have taken too much time. I didn't want to alert the cameras. That was one thing. And by the time I got in, Number Three would be awake and aware of my presence and ready to defend himself. He didn't have any weapons, unless he had some homemade ones, so I probably could have taken him out easily enough. But I didn't want to take him out. I needed him alive to test my theory.

Rather than me go in, I needed him to come out.

I thought about setting the place on fire. That would have rousted him out sure enough, but it also would have lit the entire area like a football stadium. If I started a fire, I would be visible to the cameras and Freeze would send someone to punch my ticket. A fire was out of the question.

I flicked the butane lighter and looked at my watch with the spark. 12:47. I needed to hurry. If I didn't take care of everything before daylight, I was going to die. And if I died, Juliet would die. She would have to battle Number Three or Number Six or Number Seven, and she would be no match for any of them. Juliet was five two and weighed a hundred and ten pounds soaking wet. She was feisty and had taken some kung fu training from a Chinese master in the Philippines, but she was still no match for any of those guys. Any one of them would break her like a twig. And Freeze knew it. He'd put her in the game for no other reason than to fuck with my head. So I needed to hurry.

I needed to get Number Three out of the house without torching the place and without making much noise, and I needed to do it quickly. A roaring fire was out of the question, but maybe a little smoke would do the trick. Maybe I could fill Number Three's shack with some thick smoke, and he would come out coughing and still half asleep. Then I could jump him and subdue him and do what I needed to do. It was worth a try.

I set my spear to the side and stuffed several handfuls of scrub grass into a pocket and scooted across the porch to the door. Freeze referred to these structures as *houses*, but they were built more like lawnmower sheds. Unlike the tight seal of a properly constructed home, there was a tiny gap between the threshold and the bottom of the door. When I thought about it, it was really the only ventilation in these places with the windows closed. That's probably why the builders had left the space. To allow air in and out. I crammed some of the dry grass into the gap and used one of my last six lighter ignitions to get it going. I lit one end and then stoked it by gently blowing on it. It seemed to be working. The grass started burning like tobacco in a pipe, glowing red but with no flame, and most of the smoke was being drawn into the cabin.

I was patting myself on the back, feeling pretty much like a genius, until someone from behind said, "Looking for something?"

It was Number Three. I recognized the voice. He scared the piss out of me. I literally wet my pants a little bit. A hot jolt of adrenaline flooded my nervous system and I rose and dived toward where the voice had come from and we collided with a thud and went rolling off the porch into the grass. Number Three was six five and weighed two ten. I didn't want to get into a wrestling match with him. He was way bigger than me, and I knew if he pinned me down I wouldn't stand a chance. But he didn't pin me down. The impact must have knocked the wind out of him. We rolled into the grass, and I managed to end up on top and I slammed the butt of my hand into his face hoping to break his nose. I missed. I missed completely, and I felt the edges of his front teeth dig into the skin of my palm. They sliced into the fleshy area up toward my thumb. It was going to hurt like a bitch later, but at the moment I didn't feel much of anything. Before he could shout from the pain of his incisors caving in, I covered his bloody mouth with one hand and drew my knife with the other.

I pressed the razor-sharp blade across his throat and whispered into his ear: "If you make a sound, I'm going to cut your fucking head off. Understand?"

He nodded.

"If I wanted to kill you, you'd be dead right now," I said. "I'm going to have to tie you up, but I'm going to let you live as long as you keep quiet. As long as you're quiet and don't try to resist, you get to keep breathing. OK?"

He nodded again.

I took my hand away from his mouth. "Take your shirt off," I said.

He sat up and peeled off the red jersey, and I used the knife to cut it into strips. I stuffed a piece into his mouth and tied a gag to secure it tightly and used the rest of the material to tie his wrists and ankles. I hoped the bonds would bear some thrashing. I hoped they would hold, because what I planned to do next wasn't going to be very pleasant for old Number Three. Not very pleasant at all.

I flicked my Bic and briefly ran the sharp edge of the knife along the flame.

Dr. Colt to the operating room, stat.

Dr. Colt to the operating room...

I almost started laughing. I was giddy from exhaustion and nervous as hell. I almost started laughing, but I managed to hold it together. It was certainly no laughing matter. I was about to slice into another human being. I was about to perform what amounted to an unnecessary surgical procedure, and I was doing it with no medical training and no anesthesia. Funny as a crutch, as Joe Crawford and I used to say back in sixth grade.

I walked my fingers across the top of Number Three's chest and felt for the defibrillator. I found the lump under his left collarbone. Same place as mine. It was as dark as the bottom of the ocean out there, so I had to do everything by feel. I found the lump and doused the entire area with some of the peroxide I'd brought from the first-aid kit and then poured some on my hands. I wanted to reduce the risk of infection, but I knew what

I was doing wasn't really enough. I needed some Betadine and a sterile scalpel and sterile gloves. But it probably didn't matter anyway. Number Three was probably going to bleed to death or die of shock or blow an aneurysm from the stress and pain I was about to inflict on him. And if my hunch was wrong, he was going to die from the defibrillator automatically discharging into his heart. He probably wasn't going to live long enough to get an infection.

He was moaning and shaking his head and trying to say something. He'd felt me palpating for the lump, and he'd felt the cold hydrogen peroxide being splashed on his chest. He couldn't see me, but he knew something was up. He was a doctor. A real one. He'd probably figured out what I was planning to do, and he'd probably figured out the reason. He was being used for a lab rat, and he knew it. He started thrashing and bucking and trying to make some noise, but the nylon strips from his shirt held tight and I straddled him and pressed my hand on his throat to keep his head still as I made a vertical incision along the top of the lump. Soon the metallic scent of fresh blood trumped the odor coming from his body. I fingered the warm and sticky wound and felt the metal disk implant. I felt for wires. The internal defibrillator on the Mexican information video had wires. I felt all around the disk and underneath it, but there weren't any. I yanked it out, felt again to make sure, and then whizzed it into the blackness.

Number Three was still panting and moaning, which meant he was still breathing. He was still alive. My theory had panned out. The defibrillator was nothing but a bluff. A dummy. It was the chains on the elephants, just as The Potato Man had proclaimed in my dreams. Now I could go outside the game's boundaries and not have to worry about my heart getting zapped. One less thing to stress over.

Number Three was obviously in excruciating pain, but the nylon cloth I'd stuffed into his mouth muted his screams. I poured some more of the peroxide on the open wound and dressed it with gauze and tape. It needed stitches, but a needle and thread hadn't been included in the first-aid kit. I planned to add that to my list of complaints. Not that a needle and thread would have done me or him much good. It was too dark to try to use them anyway.

At that moment, I'm sure Number Three would have killed me given the chance. What he probably didn't realize at that moment, though, was that I had done him a great favor. If things went my way, both of us would be out of this nightmare by daylight. If things went my way, Number Three would soon be thanking me for saving his life.

I leaned over and whispered into his ear again. "I have to go," I said. "But you're going to be all right. I took the defibrillator out of your chest. It was inert, just a metal disk with no wires or anything attached. Harmless. It was a bluff to keep us in line. That's all the fuck it was. You're going to be all right. I put a lot of gauze on your incision and I put pressure on it with tape, so you shouldn't lose much blood. I'm going to leave you here, and with a little luck the next faces you'll see will be a team of paramedics loading you into an ambulance."

I used the rest of the peroxide to wash the blood off my hands. I flicked the lighter and looked at my compass and headed toward the woods at a trot.

Chapter Thirty-Five

I'd been blindfolded that first day we got off the bus, when Wade had led me into the swamp with my hand on his shoulder, but it had been morning and we were in and out of the shade and I'd intermittently felt the warmth of the sun on my back the whole way. So I knew the road we'd traveled in on was east of my house, which made it southeast of Number Three's house. I knew I needed to go southeast, and I guessed it was at least a mile through the woods to the road, maybe a little more.

I went at it the same way as before, using the squirrel spear as a feeler. It was a little after two o'clock, less than four hours till sunrise. At sunrise, I would turn into a pumpkin. A dead one. The cameras would pick me up and Freeze would see I'd taken a long, unauthorized walk and it wouldn't take more than a few minutes for his guys to chase me down and do their thing. If I was seen outside the playing field, they would know that I knew the defibrillators were bogus. I was a danger to them now, and they wouldn't hesitate to execute me on the spot.

Under normal circumstances, I can easily walk a mile in thirty minutes. That's at a leisurely pace. And if I jog, I can shave that by at least a third. But these weren't normal circumstances. I was walking through fairly heavy brush, and I was doing it blind. I hadn't slept enough or eaten enough in the past few days, and the altercation with Number Three had drained most of any energy reserves I might have had on tap. I was hurting. I was running on fumes. It was going to be the longest walk of my life, and I had no idea what to expect when I reached my destination. All I could hope for was that a little luck would finally come my way.

It was a still night, no breeze and unseasonably warm and humid. I was sweating profusely, and I hadn't thought to bring any water along. Of all the things to forget. I was thirsty and feeling a little lightheaded, but I kept going. I soldiered on. I was very tired and on the verge of being dehydrated, but I knew if I stopped and sat down to rest I might never get up. If I never got up, Juliet would surely perish. I kept going. I did it for her. I did it for her and for Joe.

The woods seemed to go on forever. I checked the compass again and adjusted my course, and a few minutes later I came to a small clearing and saw the first branch of lightning streak across the sky. It lit the landscape bluely for a second, made it look like the set of a horror movie. Lightning flashed again and thunder crackled and I wished for the rain to come. I'd saved the empty peroxide bottle from the first-aid kit. If the rain came, I would be able to collect some drinking water. But it didn't come. The lightning burned the sky and the thunder boomed like a cannon, but not a drop of rain fell.

I moved quickly through the clearing, in case the storm made me visible to the cameras. It seemed the entire universe was against me now, and I felt like shaking my fist skyward and asking it why. But the universe never answers. The universe is like Number Seven, the former Navy SEAL. The universe is a professional killer. It doesn't usually say anything. It just kills you. The universe is one mean son of a bitch. I walked on.

And on.

I leaned against the gnarled trunk of a live oak, thinking this was it. My legs were like rubber. I couldn't take another step. I slid to the ground and sat on the dry underbrush with my back against the tree. I flicked the lighter. My watch said 3:17. It had been well over an hour since I'd left Number Three's house. I should have been to the road by now.

And I was.

Lightning blazed overhead, and through a stand of pine trees to my left I saw a narrow strip of blacktop about fifty feet from where I sat. Fat lengths of plastic tape had been threaded along the border of the woods, marking the boundary of the playing field. But the boundary didn't matter to me anymore. I'd proven the defibrillators were fake, which rendered the boundaries meaningless.

Now that I had made it to the road, I wasn't sure what to do. I sat there and thought about it. I looked at my compass. The strip of blacktop went north and south. One direction would lead to a bigger road and eventually to traffic and civilization. To people who could help me. To a telephone. To the police. The other direction would lead deeper into the swamp, no telling where. Either way I would be out of the playing area and therefore away from all the cameras mounted on posts and trees, but there was still the matter of the cameras embedded in the collar around my neck. The point-of-view cameras. I'd almost forgotten about them. If I went the wrong way and walked and walked until the sun came up, Freeze would see the images from the POV cameras around my neck. He would know I was far, far away from my house, from where I was supposed to be. He would know that I figured out the defibrillators were phony, and he would send his men to kill me. So I had to make a decision quickly. North or south. One direction led to potential salvation, the other to certain death.

I had a fifty-fifty chance of picking the right direction. If I could get up and walk. I thought I could probably make one last push, but what if I chose wrong? That would be it, for me and for my wife. Life and death came down to the toss of a coin. North or south? Left or right? I had no idea, but I knew I had to choose. Staying put and doing nothing was not an option. Staying put and doing nothing would amount to a zero percent chance of survival. Five more minutes, I thought. Five more minutes of rest, and I would decide.

The minutes rolled by, and I decided to head north on the road. There was no reason behind my decision. It was a random choice. One-to-one odds weren't good enough to be betting mine and Juliet's lives on, but there was no alternative. I stood up and shook off the dizziness and put one foot in front of the other.

I'd taken several steps toward the road when a pair of headlight beams rounded the corner. It was a small four-door sedan, a Camry or a Sentra or maybe one of the Korean brands. Too dark to tell for sure. It had come from the south, but that didn't tell me much of anything. It could have come from the main highway, where I wanted to go, or it could have come from somewhere else in the swamp. The Okefenokee contained a land mass of almost half a million acres. The car could have come from anywhere.

The driver pulled to the side of the road and opened the door and got out. He left the headlights on and the engine running. I could see his silhouette. It appeared to be one of the guys wearing blue coveralls and a red ball cap. One of the maintenance guys. He switched on a flashlight and walked a few feet beyond the shoulder to a post topped with a rectangular steel box. He pulled out a ring of keys and opened the door to the hollow metal housing. It was about the size of a shoebox. I figured maybe it was some sort of junction for the cameras. He made a lot of noise jingling his keys and fiddling with getting the door open. He wasn't trying to be quiet. He thought he was alone. I was cloaked by the woods, and he had no idea I was standing there spying on him.

I wanted his car. I needed it, and I needed for him to tell me the way back to civilization.

I pulled out my nunchucks and crept toward him, treading as lightly as I could. He had a walkie-talkie on his belt, but otherwise appeared to be weaponless. He was concentrating on the junction box. He never heard me coming. I used the chain from the nunchucks like a garrote, choking him tightly enough to keep him from talking but not enough to completely occlude his airway. I didn't want to kill him yet. I needed him to give me directions.

He fell to his knees. Made some little mewling sounds. I stayed upright behind him, holding the handles to the nunchucks the way you would hold a pair of post-hole diggers. I loosened the tension slightly and whispered for him to be quiet. I told him to shut the fuck up or I was going to break his windpipe. He nodded in agreement. We had a deal. I loosened the grip some more, but not enough for him to wriggle out of it.

"Which way to the highway?" I said.

"You think I'm stupid? If I tell you, you won't need me anymore. You'll kill me."

"Maybe, maybe not. But I'm sure as shit going to kill you if you don't tell me."

He was wheezing from the pressure on his trachea. He knew he was going to die if he didn't say something. "You have to go south a couple of miles, and then veer left at the fork. Another ten miles and you'll see some lights, and then you'll see the signs to the interstate."

"I'm going to take you with me," I said. "I'm going to stuff your ass into the trunk and take you with me. If you're lying, I'm going to tie you to the bumper of the car and drag you all the way back here. Then the buzzards can have whatever's left of your corpse."

"I swear. You have to go south and then southwest. Left at the fork."

"Stand up," I said.

He stood. I pulled the chain a little tighter against his throat and started walking backward toward the idling sedan. I walked him to the driver's side and told him to open the door. He did.

"Reach in there and cut the engine," I said.

He reached in and cut the engine. I still had the nunchuck chain tight against his windpipe.

"Now take the keys out of the ignition."

He took the keys out of the ignition. I was going to make him open the trunk, and then I was going to slam the lid and imprison him once he was inside. If he'd told me wrong on the directions, I planned to make good on my promise to drag his worthless carcass back to our current position. If he'd told me correctly, I planned to hand him over to the cops. Either way, he was going to lose. Everyone involved in this fucked-up world Freeze had created was going to lose. I planned to make sure of it.

I guided him to the rear of the car. "Open the trunk," I said.

But he didn't. He reared back and launched the keys to the other side of the road and at the same time came down hard on the instep of my left foot. The shock of the sudden crunching pain shot up my spinal cord and briefly paralyzed my fingers on that side. There had been some nerve damage in my left hand after the trauma in Tennessee anyway, and the strength in my ring finger and pinky had never returned a hundred percent. The paralysis only lasted a second, but it was enough time for him to wriggle free and take off running.

If he had been thinking straight, he could have started screaming and shouting and whooping and hollering. He could have started making a lot of noise, and the cameras would have picked up the ruckus and alerted whoever was monitoring them that something was terribly wrong. Then whoever was monitoring the cameras could have cranked on some lights, which would have immediately revealed good old Number Eight Nicholas Colt standing there with his ass flapping in the nonexistent breeze.

But the guy wasn't thinking straight. He didn't start screaming and shouting and whooping and hollering. He just ran. My left hand was a little numb, and the top of my foot felt like someone had taken a sledgehammer to it. My right hand hurt. It was skinned and bruised from hitting Number Three in the teeth.

But it still worked OK.

I pulled my knife from its sheath and whizzed it at him overhand like a tomahawk. It thudded deeply into his back, just below his right rib cage. He fell to the pavement. Curled into a fetal position. Started moaning and writhing. I hobbled to where he lay and kicked the knife around a few times with the toe of my boot. I wanted to make sure he was good and sliced up inside. I kicked it around a few times and then yanked it out and watched him bleed. Stupid motherfucker. He should have just cooperated. I didn't have time for this shit.

I took his flashlight and walked back to the car. I crossed the road and descended an embankment and looked around for the keys. I followed a line to where I thought they might be. I got lucky. I spotted them in the mud twenty feet or so from the road.

I spotted them, but there was a problem.

Below the keys, where the embankment ended and the water began, from the stagnant black cypress stump soup people ordinarily associate with the word *swamp*, a pair of bloodred eyes stared hungrily back at me.

Chapter Thirty-Six

Gators. Of course. What else?

I swept the area with the flashlight. There were four of them. Four sentinels armed with jaws powerful enough to rip a grown man's arm clean off with a single snap. Four slimy smelly ugly sons of bitches from darkest prehistoric hell.

Their tails and hind legs were submerged, with their front halves resting happily on the mucky bank. They all looked up at me. They all wore that shit-eating alligator grin, as if they were daring me to come on down. As if they were daring me to cross an imaginary line.

"Run along, fellas," I whispered. "I won't hurt you if you don't hurt me."

They stood their ground. Kept grinning. I took that as a "Fuck you, bubba. You want these keys, you're going to have to go through us to get them."

I wanted those keys. I needed them. Those keys represented victory for me and defeat for Freeze. All I had to do was start the car and find the interstate and pull off at the first exit. Stop at a filling station and phone the police. Game over. Freeze goes to prison, Juliet and I live happily ever after.

With the car, I had plenty of time to do what I needed to do before daylight. Without the car, I wasn't going to make it. I didn't have the time or the energy to walk twelve miles. Even if I could have somehow mustered the strength, the sun would have risen on me somewhere between my current position and the interstate. The sun would rise and the cameras in my collar would give me away, and that would be that. Game over. Freeze keeps kidnapping people and hosting his demented sport every year, and Juliet and I get buried somewhere in the Okefenokee Swamp.

I needed those keys, but I couldn't very well wrestle four alligators to get them. Four gators that I could see, and there might be more lurking nearby. There might be a dozen of them for all I knew. One slip and they would all converge and tear me apart. It was an impossible situation. If I went for the keys, the gators would kill me. If I didn't go for the keys, Freeze would kill me. My only choice seemed to be which way I wanted to die.

Then I got an idea.

I climbed up the hill and walked north on the road a hundred feet or so and then climbed back down. I switched on the flashlight and looked around.

No gators in sight.

I turned the light off and crept southward toward where I'd been before, back toward the ruthless predators standing guard over the keys. I was hoping they might have gotten bored and moved on, but they were still there. Still half in the water, half out. The original four were still there, and now a fifth had joined them. A smaller one. A youngster.

I got as close as I dared, and then I pulled out the stun baton. My plan was to shock all the gators by shocking the water. I figured the voltage might paralyze them long enough for me to snatch the car keys and make a run for it. Or it might do nothing. I didn't know.

It was a risk, because discharging the stun baton would then render it useless. That would mean one less weapon in my arsenal. Also, my boots were in the mud now and I wondered if I would get shocked myself. The boots had rubber soles, so I didn't think so. I decided to give it a shot. If it didn't work, I would have to think of something else. I had to have those car keys no matter what.

I bent down, put my finger on the trigger, and fired the baton into the water. I expected to see some fireworks. I expected blue arcs of electrical current to explode into the bog and light up the night. But nothing happened. Nothing happened, and the gators didn't move.

I picked up a large rock and hurled it toward the pack of monsters and switched on the flashlight. They still didn't move. I wondered if they were dead.

I trudged along the muddy bank toward them, keeping the light aimed at the keys. One of them opened its mouth in what looked like a yawn, but it didn't stir from its position. The stun baton had temporarily paralyzed those ghastly fucking creatures from the black lagoon, just as I had predicted.

I walked to within three feet of them, bent over, and reached for the keys.

Chapter Thirty-Seven

I was inches from wrapping my fingers around surefire salvation when the baby of the bunch darted from nowhere and snapped at my hand. I got out of the way in time, but the scummy little bastard scooped the shiny ring into its mouth and raised its head in a thrashing motion and swallowed the keys in a single gulp.

"Motherfucker," I said.

I pulled my knife and went after him. He was only about three feet long. I figured I could handle him. I figured I could stab him in the brain and then slit his belly open and retrieve the keys. He made a hissing sound, and our eyes locked and I was about to come down overhand and plant the blade into his skull when one of the larger animals started edging its way out of the mire. First one, and then another. And another. And another. They were all waking up from the stun gun shock. It was no longer just me against the runt. It was back to one against five.

I took a step backward, and they all came after me. I turned and ran as fast as I could, climbing the embankment at an angle. I didn't look back until I got to the car.

Fortunately, the gators gave up somewhere along the way.

Unfortunately, I still didn't have the keys. I didn't have them, and I wasn't going to get them.

I looked at my watch. 4:21. I had wasted over an hour trying to get the car, first from the guy in blue coveralls and a red ball cap, and then from the alligators. And I had failed. Now it was less than two hours till daybreak. Now I was screwed.

I should have killed the maintenance man in the first place. I never should have spoken to him. I should have just crept up from behind and severed one of the arteries in his neck. He would have bled out and died in under a minute, and I would have had the keys. I hadn't known which way to go, north or south, but I could have tried both ways. I had had time to try both ways. I could have skipped the coercion. That's the way it should have gone down. If it had, maybe I would be in a nice soft bed by now with a hot meal in front of me.

But then hindsight's always twenty-twenty. I needed to forget about what could have happened, what should have happened. I needed to forget about it and move on. My chances of surviving now were slim to none, but I needed to accept that and move on to Plan B.

Plan B wasn't much of a plan at all. If what the maintenance man had said was true, the interstate was about twelve miles south of my current position. It was way too late to even think about walking that far now, so my only other real choice was to travel north. I had no idea what waited in that direction. The maintenance man hadn't said, and I hadn't thought to ask. I was too busy basking in the glow of victory at the time, sure I was going to momentarily be speeding along the blacktop, the metaphorical yellow brick road to home. Rule #23 in Nicholas Colt's *Philosophy of Life*: Don't count your chickens before they hatch. It's a cliché, but a good one. I felt like a fool for celebrating too soon.

I decided to take a few minutes to go through the car, thinking there might be something of use stowed in the glove box or under one of the seats. The first thing I saw when I opened the driver's-side door was a bottle of Zephyrhills spring water in the center console drink caddy. I grabbed it and screwed the cap off and chugged it like no tomorrow. The bottle was over half full, and I drank every bit of it. It was like finding a magic elixir. Manna from heaven. It immediately kicked my energy level up a notch. I drank every drop and then tossed the empty plastic bottle to the backseat.

I rummaged through the glove compartment. There was an owner's manual and a vehicle registration and a couple of receipts from oil changes and three peppermint disks wrapped in cellophane. I snatched the candy and unwrapped one and popped it in my mouth and stuffed the other two in a pocket.

I reached under the bucket seat on the driver's side, pulled out a Dr Pepper bottle cap and a petrified french fry. I looked at the fry, thought about it, flicked it into the grass. I reached under the seat on the passenger's side and right away felt the unmistakable shape and texture and beautiful coldness of something way too good to be true.

I pulled it out and looked at it with the flashlight. It was a Walther 9mm semiautomatic. I prefer revolvers, but the Walther was a very nice pistol. I checked the magazine. It held eight rounds, and it was full. The gun fit easily into my front pocket.

I gently closed the car door and started walking north. I had three weapons again, the nunchucks, the knife, and now the 9mm. I had in essence traded the stun baton for the pistol. It was a good trade. The stun baton was one of the best weapons given out in Snuff Tag 9, but of course a handgun was far superior in almost any situation. And I wasn't out to stun anybody at this point. I was out to kill them dead. I was out to kill them while expending as little energy as possible. The pistol was a godsend. After all the bad luck I'd had, it seemed like things were finally turning around.

But I still had no idea where I was going.

I didn't walk on the road itself. I stayed off to the side, near the tree line. If a vehicle came from either direction, I would have time to duck into the woods before I was spotted.

4:32.

I popped another peppermint, hoping the sugar would help sustain the energy boost I'd gotten from the big drink of water. I felt OK. I was limping a little from where the maintenance man had stomped my foot, and my hand hurt from where I'd knocked Number Three's teeth out, but otherwise I felt like a million bucks. I felt like I could walk a hundred miles if I needed to.

I felt OK, but the clock was my worst enemy now. I had weapons and I felt good, but time was running out. Less than an hour and a half till sunrise. I started walking a little faster, just because it seemed like the thing to do.

I heard something rustling in the brush, swept the area with the flashlight, and saw a fox creeping stealthily through the woods. He stopped and stared into the light for a few seconds and then darted away. I wondered what else was lurking about. Every few minutes I shone the light into the woods, hoping the next creature I encountered wasn't a panther or a bear or something. Some sort of predator that might look at me and see prime rib. The experience with the alligators had me a little paranoid about wildlife in the swamp.

I felt the collar on my neck, thought about trying to cut it off. Frederick had said it was rigged with an alarm, but that might have been as big a bluff as the defibrillators. I decided not to risk it just yet. Maybe closer to sunrise. Alarm or not, Freeze—or whoever was monitoring the cameras at the moment—would know something was up, but at least they wouldn't have a video feed to my exact location.

The narrow strip of blacktop seemed to snake on to infinity. I walked at a brisk pace for twenty more minutes and then slowed down a bit. Finally I stopped completely. I just stood there. Shone the flashlight up the road to nowhere. I was getting tired again. And thirsty. I wanted to just lie down and fall asleep. Five minutes, I thought. Five minutes of sleep and I would be a new man. I wished I hadn't guzzled all the water at once. I wished I had sipped it a little at a time. If I had been more sparing with it, I would still have some.

Another mistake.

It seemed all I was capable of anymore was fucking up. I figured I was going to die in a little while. It was almost a certainty now. The road was too long and time was too short. I thought about what my obituary might say: *Nicholas Colt, once a world-class musician, then an ace private detective, and finally a first-rate fuck-up, died today of utter stupidity...*

Of course I probably wouldn't even get an obituary, not for years anyway, because they would probably never find my body. Juliet and I would be buried somewhere on Freeze's property, never to be heard from again. Juliet and I would spend eternity rotting in unmarked graves, and Freeze would start the selection process for next year's round of Snuff Tag 9. Somehow it just didn't seem fair.

I was on the verge of falling asleep standing up. I took a deep breath. I heard a rustling sound in the woods again, and again I swept the area with the flashlight. I didn't see any animals this time, but I saw something else, something in the distance.

I ducked under the border tape and walked a few feet into the woods to check it out.

The pain in my right hand had gotten worse, so I switched the flashlight to my left. I thought my eyes were playing tricks on me, but they weren't. A structure about the size of a lawn mower shed stood fifty yards or so from the boundary. It was a house for one of the players. One of the dead ones, I hoped. If the place was vacant, I could get some water and maybe even something to eat.

I'd been to Number Three's house, and I'd left him tied up on the ground outside of it. He was there resting quietly, recovering from his little surgical procedure, so I knew this place wasn't his. The only other players still alive were Number Six and Number Seven. If the house belonged to either of them, the trek through the woods would be a waste of precious time. I couldn't very well just politely knock on one of their doors, like a neighbor asking for a cup of sugar. I couldn't confront them in any way, because doing that would alert Freeze and the boys that I wasn't where I was supposed to be. No, if the house belonged to Number Six or Number Seven, I would have to backtrack to where I was now. It would be a waste of time, but even so I figured the entire mission wouldn't take more than ten minutes. It was worth the risk, especially since I didn't know what to expect on the road ahead anyway. It was worth the risk just for a chance at a drink of water.

All I could hope for was that the house belonged to one of the players who had already been killed.

I crept deeper into the woods. When I got close enough, I switched off the flashlight and belly-crawled the rest of the way to the front porch. It was too dark to see, and I didn't want to use the light, so I stood and felt the brass number tacked to the left support post.

The house didn't belong to Number Six, and it didn't belong to Number Seven.

And it didn't belong to any of the dead players.

The house belonged to Number Nine.

It was Juliet's house.

I cupped my hands and peeked into the window, saw only blackness. I switched on the flashlight for a brief second and shone it inside. The bed was empty. The house was still vacant. They hadn't brought her here yet. Probably later this morning, blindfolded, the same way they'd delivered the rest of us.

I opened the door and walked in. My first stop was the faucet. I turned it on, bent down, and slurped from the stream. I rinsed my face and my hair and then slurped some more. When I'd had enough, I uncapped the hydrogen peroxide bottle and rinsed it out and filled it. I wished I'd kept the Zephyrhills bottle from the maintenance man's car, but back then I'd doubted I was going to live long enough to need it anyway. Maybe it was better that I hadn't kept it. Less weight in my backpack.

I thought about what to do next. I thought about waiting there for Juliet to come and then killing her escort, but that was no good. The sun would come up before then, and the cameras would spot me and alert Freeze to my location. I would die, and Juliet would die. I couldn't stick around. I had to get back to the road and keep heading north. I didn't know where it would take me, but I knew it would take me somewhere. Maybe it would take me to Juliet, and maybe I could rescue her before they even brought her out here.

But if the road didn't take me to Juliet, if I wasn't able to rescue her before they brought her to this house, she would soon be forced to battle either Number Six or Number Seven. In either case, she would surely be killed.

I sat on the bed for a few minutes and thought about everything, about all the potential outcomes. At that moment, it was all still a mystery. At that moment, everything was still uncertain. But days later I would learn about everything that had happened. All the horrible details. Days later, I would learn that at the exact moment I was sitting there on the bed in the shack thinking about how we might possibly make it out of this nightmare alive, the lights in Juliet's room at Freeze's house came on. The lights came on, and a voice came over the intercom.

"Good morning, dear," Freeze said. "I trust you slept well."

"Fuck you," Juliet said. "I didn't sleep much at all. But you probably already know that, don't you. You fucking prick. You

probably have hidden cameras here in my room, and you probably saw me tossing and turning all night."

"Such a mouth on you. So feisty, just like your husband. Did
he teach you those bad words?"

"Fuck you."

"Yes, well, at any rate, you need to get up and get ready now.
Your escort will be there soon."

Juliet got up and got ready. She knew she didn't have a choice.
If she refused to obey, Freeze would zap her heart with the defibrillator. Her only chance was to do what she was told, to play the
game and hope for the best.

She brushed her teeth and put on the black fatigue pants and
the boots and the red number 9 jersey. She stowed her weapons—
a can of pepper spray and a set of brass knuckles—into the side
flap pockets on her pants. She looked in the mirror. With the
G-29 transceiver attached to her ear and the cam-collar wrapped
around her neck, she looked like some sort of futuristic soccer
mom.

A few minutes after she got dressed, Wade came in and led
her blindfolded to the elevator.

Chapter Thirty-Eight

I walked back out to the tree line and continued following the road north.

5:16.

I unwrapped the last peppermint and popped it in my mouth. The long drink at Juliet's house had revived me somewhat, but I was still very fatigued. On my last leg. Rode hard and put up wet. Tired as a motherfucker.

I walked for almost twenty minutes, and then the road ran out. It just stopped, as if the construction budget had been exhausted. I walked to the edge, noticed a rutted path that led into a heavily forested area. I followed the path for about a quarter of a mile and came to a steel gate secured with a padlock. A sign said WARNING: NO TRESPASSING. I ignored it and climbed over the gate. What were they going to do, arrest me? I should be so lucky.

The goat path continued on the other side of the gate and eventually turned into the concrete driveway of a house. Single level with an attached garage. There was a ten-speed bicycle chained to the porch railing but no cars parked outside.

I crept to the garage door and gently lifted the handle. It was wet with dew and locked. I needed to get inside. If there was a vehicle in there, I needed to find the keys and steal it. I needed to steal it and put the pedal to the metal. With a car, there was still enough time to make it to the interstate before daylight. With a car, there was still hope. And even if there wasn't a car in the garage, maybe there was a telephone in there or in the house. A landline. One phone call and the cavalry would be on the way. Adrenaline flooded my brain. I could feel my pulse in my face. This was it. I could feel it. One way or another, this house was going to provide what I needed to save my wife and myself. One way or another, we were going to be out of this mess soon.

All I had to do was get inside.

I walked the perimeter of the house, checking all the windows. I figured the bicycle belonged to somebody, and I figured that somebody was probably in one of the bedrooms asleep. I wanted to get inside without waking him or her up, so I was doing everything as quietly as possible. I was going at it like some kind of cat burglar. I finally found an unsecured window in back. I tapped the flashlight's button for a second and peered in through a set of sheer curtains. On the other side of the window were a wooden table and four chairs. It was the dining room. Perfect. I only hoped the house didn't have an alarm system. Or a dog. If a dog started barking, I was screwed. It didn't matter. I had to go for it.

I cut the screen out with my knife, raised the window on its tracks, climbed inside. So far, so good. No dog and no alarm. I switched the flashlight on and cupped my hand over it to keep the light low. It was an open floor plan, with the dining room leading to the kitchen. There was a closed door on the far side of the kitchen, and from the layout outside I knew it had to lead to the garage. I searched for a set of keys, all the while scanning walls and surfaces for a telephone. I looked on the dining room table and the kitchen countertop and the breakfast bar. If this had been my house, those are the places I might have thrown my car keys when I walked in. No luck. I checked the wall by the door to the garage for hooks or nails where the owner might have hung a key ring, but I struck out there as well. No keys, no phone.

I opened the door to the garage, applying upward pressure on the knob so the hinges wouldn't squeak. Maybe someone out here in the middle of nowhere wouldn't even bother taking the keys out of the ignition, I thought. Maybe the keys were still in the car. I was optimistic with the possibility until I swept the garage with the flashlight and saw that there wasn't even a fucking car in there.

No car, but there were some other things of interest.

There was a concrete floor with oil stains on it and a lawn mower draped with clear plastic and a Ping-Pong table folded up and rolled to the side. There was a wooden chair in the middle of the room, with a Japanese samurai sword mounted on the wall several feet behind it.

This was where they had killed Nathan Broadway.

And Joe Crawford.

I stepped into the garage and quietly undraped the lawn mower. As I'd hoped, there was a gasoline can sitting on the floor beside it. It was a one-gallon can. Metal. Red and gold. I picked it up and shook it. It was over half full.

I carried the can of gasoline into the house and crept down the hallway to the bedrooms. There were three. Two on the left side of the hallway and one on the right. The first door on the left was open. I cupped my hand over the flashlight, switched it on, and walked in. There was a mattress on the floor and a wooden orange crate topped with an ashtray full of butts. Someone had tried to mask the smell of dirty linen and cigarette smoke with air freshener and had failed.

I walked back out to the hallway. The other bedroom door on the left was closed, as was the one on the right. I cupped my ear against the one on the left and then the one on the right. Someone was snoring behind the one on the right. I gently opened the door on the left to make sure the room was vacant, and it was.

I unscrewed the cap from the gasoline can and stealthily entered the snoring man's chamber. I'd switched off the flashlight, but the blue glow from the digital alarm clock on the nightstand illuminated the room well enough to navigate. A pair of pants had been hung on one of the bedposts and a sleeveless white T-shirt on the other. I felt the pants with my fingertips. Leather, as I'd suspected. The man lying in front of me comfortably sawing logs had tortured and killed my oldest and dearest friend in the world. I stared at his sleeping figure for a minute and tried to process that. Tried to wrap my head around the utter senselessness of it all. The absurdity. Joe Crawford hadn't done anything to warrant that sort of treatment. His only crime was being my friend, and he had paid the ultimate price for it.

Now it was this motherfucker's turn to pay. Leather Pants was fixing to die, and I was prepared to die with him if necessary.

I stood over him and lifted the can and drenched him head-to-toe with gasoline. He sputtered and gasped and started trying to kick the sheets off. He wasn't quite awake yet. Maybe he thought he was in the middle of a nightmare, which in fact he was.

"Wake up, you piece of shit," I said.

He opened his eyes and started coughing and grunting. "Who are you?" he said. "What do you want? How dare you—"

"Shut the fuck up. Shut the fuck up, and take a whiff of Jif. You smell that? What's it smell like?"

"Oh my god," he said. "It's gasoline. You poured gasoline all over me."

The room was thick with volatile vapors, and old Leather Pants sounded like he was about to start crying.

"Bingo," I said. "Gasoline. You're not quite as stupid as you look. There's still a little in the can, but I poured most of it on you. About half a gallon. Enough to cook your ass good and proper if you don't tell me what I need to know."

He was trembling all over. He gripped one of his pillows tight against his chest, as if it might grow legs and run away if he let go. "Whatever you want, man. I have money. I have gold necklaces and bracelets on the dresser over there. Take whatever you want. Really, I—"

"Shut up!" I shouted. "I don't want any of your goddamn shit. If I wanted it, I would have taken it. Now listen. You're going to tell me how to get to Freeze's house, and you're going to tell me where to find the key to the lock on that bicycle outside."

"The key's in my pants pocket. On the bedpost."

I reached over and transferred the set of keys from his pocket to mine.

"Where's your cell phone?" I said.

"I don't have one."

"Everybody has a cell phone. Tell me where the fuck it is."

"It's on the dresser, man. But it won't do you any good. There's no signal out here."

I felt around on the dresser, picked up the phone, and turned it on. He was telling the truth. There was no signal, not one bar.

"How do I get to the mansion?" I said.

"Who are you?"

I pulled my knife and raised it like a hatchet and came down hard on his right leg just above the foot. I felt the blade sink into his shinbone. I had to yank on it pretty hard to dislodge it. He screamed and let go of the pillow and held his knee to his chest with his hands wrapped around the wound.

"You think I'm fucking playing?" I said. "Tell me what I want to know, or I'm going to start chopping shit off."

"I can't tell you that. I can't. I just can't. Oh god. You cut me, motherfucker. You cut me really bad."

He was whining like a kid who'd scraped his knee. Boo fucking hoo. I put the knife away and pulled out the butane lighter.

"You know what this is?" I said. "Maybe you can't see it. It's kind of dark in here, and maybe your vision is a little blurred from the tears and the gasoline fumes. Maybe you can't see what I'm holding, so allow me to describe it for you. It's red and shiny and about three inches long. No, it's not your dick. But hey, it rhymes with dick. It's a Bic! That's right. A disposable cigarette lighter. I think they've been around since sometime in the early seventies. I'm sure you've seen one before. There's a plastic oval-shaped fuel reservoir and a flint wheel and a little lever you hold down with your thumb when you want the spark to ignite the butane. It makes a nice one-inch flame, blue at the bottom and orange at the top."

I was being dramatic as hell, enjoying watching him squirm.

"You won't light that," he said. "If you light that, this whole fucking house will go up in flames. It'll go up like the goddamn *Hindenburg*. If you light that lighter, you'll burn right along with me."

I flicked the flint wheel with my thumb. We didn't blow up. The fumes must not have been as heavy as they seemed. He saw the spark and cowered back against the headboard.

"You must have me confused with someone who's afraid to die," I said. "I'm going to ask you one more time. How do I get to Freeze's house? Tell me now, or the next time I flick my Bic we both get roasted like marshmallows."

I held the lighter to the gasoline-soaked sheets while he thought it over.

Chapter Thirty-Nine

Juliet took the elevator with Wade to the first floor, put her hand on his shoulder, and followed him outside. It was warm, but it didn't feel as though the sun had risen yet. They walked forty-three steps to a vehicle with the engine running.

"This is the transport van," Wade said. "I'm going to guide you into the backseat. Don't worry, I'll be riding with you all the way to the game site."

"OK," Juliet said.

Wade guided her into the backseat, sat beside her, slid the door shut.

"Good morning, Jon," Wade said.

"Morning," the driver said.

Juliet felt the transmission shift into gear. The van lurched forward. She kept hoping that this was all part of some bizarre nightmare, that she would wake up in her bed at home and smell Nicholas's bad coffee brewing.

Nicholas.

She wondered if he was even still alive. She hoped that he was. She wanted to tell him that all was forgiven, that he could come home now and they could be a family again. She'd longed for his touch for so long. She'd deprived herself of the best love she'd ever known, all because of pride. She'd blamed it on the tradition of her family's culture, but it really boiled down to the useless emotions of pride and jealousy. How she wished she could have those months back, all those months she'd spent alone crying in her pillow at night. How she wished it was all just a bad dream.

But it wasn't a dream. This was really happening. She was riding in a van to an undisclosed location where she would play a game of kill or be killed.

Snuff Tag 9.

Wasn't that originally some sort of video game? She thought she remembered seeing it behind one of the glass cases at Walmart one time when she and Brittney were browsing the electronics department. Yes, she was sure of it. It was a game for PlayStation or Xbox or one of those systems the kids liked, and apparently this monster who called himself Freeze had become obsessed with it and had turned it into a contest among real live people. Insane. There was no other word for it. Snuff Tag 9 was utterly insane.

They rode in silence for a while, and then Wade quizzed her on some of the rules.

"What happens if you're caught using a weapon during a period when they've been prohibited?" he said.

"Immediate termination," Juliet said. "No warning."

Being a registered nurse, Juliet knew a little about automatic internal defibrillators. Cardiologists implanted them in patients with histories of deadly abhorrent heart rhythms, specifically ventricular fibrillation. The electronic device would detect the abnormality and then correct it with a mild shock to the cardiac muscle. That was how it was supposed to work. But the one that had been sewn into Juliet's chest was not a lifesaving device. Just the opposite. It was there to make her heart abruptly stop beating if she didn't do what she was told to do.

She had to hand it to Freeze. It was actually a very clever way to force compliance. Nobody wanted to die, which made it practically failsafe. The only way to escape the game was through certain death.

Not that it mattered much. She was going to die soon anyway. Freeze had shown her pictures of the players still in the game and had told her their backgrounds. They were all men, all intelligent and athletic. She would fight. She would give it her all, but she doubted she stood a chance.

Freeze had refused to give her any information about Nicholas. When she had asked, all he would say was something about not spoiling the surprise. Juliet hoped with all her heart Nicholas was still alive and that he would somehow come to her rescue. And if he could not, she prayed that he would be the one to win the game.

Chapter Forty

I flicked the flint wheel again. We didn't blow up again.

We didn't blow up, but the unmistakable tang of urine somehow cut through the gasoline vapors and briefly assaulted my olfactory nerve. Leather Pants had pissed himself.

"All right," he whimpered. "You win, man. Please, I don't want to burn. I don't want to die. Please don't strike that fucking lighter again. I'll tell you whatever you want."

He started bawling.

"Talk to me, douche bag," I said.

He told me, in great detail, how to get to Freeze's estate. It wasn't far. If I hurried, I could still make it there before daybreak.

I pulled my knife from its sheath and came down hard on his left leg, same as I'd done to his right. He screamed, but I wasn't listening. I was numb to it. He was totally crippled now. He was helpless, crying and screaming and pleading for mercy. I heard it, but none of it registered as coming from a human being. It was coming from a demon, and I was going to send its worthless ass back to hell where it belonged.

I walked out of the bedroom and drizzled the remaining gasoline on the carpet as I backed down the hallway. I flicked the lighter, depressing the little pedal that opened the fuel valve this time, but nothing happened. No flame. I tried again. Nothing. I stood there flicking and cursing, but the damn thing wouldn't light. Freeze must have been wrong about how much fuel there was, or maybe I'd used too much sterilizing the knife for Number Three's surgery.

I tossed the lighter aside and trotted into the kitchen. Switched the flashlight on and set it against the backsplash on the countertop. I didn't want a lot of light, worried it might activate my cam-collar. I opened a bunch of drawers and cabinets and flung a bunch of pots and pans and cooking utensils and Tupperware and canned goods out to the floor. Finally I found what I was looking for in the drawer by the toaster: Diamond brand strike-on-box large kitchen matches. Two hundred fifty count.

All I needed was one.

I went back to the edge of the hallway. Struck a match against the side of the box. It flared and lit the dark and narrow path orange, tinting the air with the acrid scent of sulfur. Leather Pants had rolled out of bed and was crawling toward me on his elbows. Coughing, wheezing, drooling. He looked up at me. Looked me straight in the eye. Pleading. I tossed the match on the floor, and a trail of blue fire sped toward him, and in less than a second he was engulfed in a roaring inferno. He shrieked in agony. I watched him roll around and try to put himself out, but it was no use. His skin and nightclothes were saturated with gasoline. It would have taken a fire hose to extinguish him. His face bubbled and then blackened and then melted away like candle wax.

In a final tortured spasm, his upper body rose at an impossible angle. Like a cobra being charmed out of a basket. His mouth opened in a silent scream, and his eyeballs exploded and splattered the wall with viscous bloody goo. He fell facedown and sizzled like bacon in a skillet.

The flames quickly climbed the doorjamb to the master bedroom and then got sucked in by the gasoline vapors. There was a bright orange flash and the sound of glass shattering, and I knew I needed to get out fast. If I didn't get out fast, I was going to be crispy dead just like old Leather Pants.

Before I reached the front door, a pair of smoke alarms started wailing in unison. I hoped there weren't any cameras in the area that might pick up the squeal before I had time to get away. I didn't think so. The house was at least half a mile from the perimeter of the playing field. It was at least half a mile from the field, but Leather Pants had been correct in his assessment. The whole place was going to go up like the goddamn *Hindenburg*. It wouldn't take long for someone to notice the flames and the smoke.

And that's what I was counting on.

Chapter Forty-One

I darted outside, fumbled with the keys, finally found the right one. I opened the padlock, yanked the cable loose and tossed it aside, climbed onto the bicycle, and started pedaling like my ass was on fire. Which it would have been if I hadn't gotten out of there when I did. When I got to the gate, I dismounted and found the key to open that lock, walked the bike to the other side, closed the gate and secured it, and climbed back on and rode away.

I followed the rutted path to the road. I figured it was about a ten-minute ride to Freeze's mansion if I pedaled fast.

I pedaled fast.

The faintest hint of orange had started to peek over the horizon. It didn't matter now. I was going to make it. I would be on the lot of the big house before anyone knew what was happening. I would be there before they found out I'd left my cabin, before they knew I had discovered the defibrillators were fake, before they were privy to the fact I had escaped the perimeter of the playing field. I wasn't sure what I was going to do when I got there, but I was going to make it. Somehow I was going to get them before they got me. I only hoped I could bring them down before they forced Juliet into the game.

"Good morning, Number Eight."

Fuck. It was Freeze's voice on the G-29.

"Good morning," I said, trying not to betray the fact I was huffing down the road on a ten-speed mountain bike. I was on a slight downward incline, so I stopped pedaling and coasted awhile.

"Why are you breathing so hard?" Freeze said.

"I just woke up from a bad dream. I seem to be having a lot of those lately."

"So sorry to hear that. Anyway, I wanted to give you an idea of what's in store for you today. It's going to be busy, so I want you to go ahead and get up now and get ready."

I gently braked the bike to a stop. I didn't want him to catch wind of the tires humming on the pavement.

"I'm listening," I said.

"There will be three battles today. The first two will be you against Number Six, and Number Seven against Number Three. Number Seven should win easily, and since you have a stun baton now I'm predicting you will win against Number Six. If that's the way it happens, you'll be facing Number Seven in the third battle of the day. Whoever wins that one will face Number Nine tomorrow."

Trying to hide my relief that Juliet wasn't going to have to play today, I said, "Number Nine is my wife, Freeze. Even if I win both matches today, do you really think I'm going to kill her tomorrow?"

"You will battle her as you would any other player. If you refuse, I'll make you watch her die a very slow and painful death. If you commit suicide, which I'm sure has crossed your mind, your wife will still die a very slow and painful death. And your daughter will join her."

Nobody's going to die a slow and painful death but you, moth-erfucker, I thought.

Silence for a few seconds.

"I guess I'll do what I have to do," I said.

"That's what I wanted to hear. Now—"

In the background I heard someone say, "Freeze! There's smoke coming from section seven. A lot of it. Looks like the house over there might be on fire."

"What the fuck?" Freeze said.

I heard some shoes clomping on hardwood and some other general commotion, and then the G-29 went dead. I started pedaling again, rode about half a mile, and veered off onto a hilly dirt path that snaked through the woods. The mountain bike was at home on the terrain, but my legs weren't. The tops of my thighs felt like they were on fire. I didn't have much off-road experience, and I couldn't find the right gears to make the ride tolerable. I finally had to stop and climb off and abandon the bike.

The sun had risen completely, and there was plenty of light now to see by. There was also plenty of light to activate the cam-collar, and I heard it come to life with its telltale electronic microbeep. Fuck it. I pulled my knife from its sheath and worked it under the collar and sliced through the plastic housing and the wiring and tossed the whole ruined shebang into the woods. Maybe an alarm would sound. Maybe they would know I'd taken the collar off, but at least they wouldn't be able to look at the monitor and see my exact location. If indeed anyone was even watching the monitors or listening for alarms. I was hoping every available hand was rushing to section seven to put out the fire I'd started. The amount of smoke it was producing would draw the kind of attention Freeze definitely didn't want, so I was counting on most of his staff leaving the big house and tending to the blaze before it spread and got totally out of hand.

Sweat trickled down my neck and stung the sore spots where the collar had been. I kept walking and walking. I thought I should have been there by now, and it suddenly occurred to me that Leather Pants could have purposely given me bad directions. What did he have to lose, after all? Surely he didn't think I was actually going to let him live. He could have given me directions that led to a trap or to nowhere at all. I thought about turning back and getting the bicycle and riding the thirteen miles or whatever it was to the interstate. Now that I knew Juliet was off the hook for the day, and now that the fire was providing a distraction for a good portion of Freeze's staff, I thought I might have time to do that. Then again, all the cameras were active now, and it would only take one person to realize I wasn't wearing the collar anymore. Once they realized that, they would discover I was out of my house and they would start looking for me. And they might do something to Juliet in retaliation.

I walked on slowly, trying to decide whether or not to go back for the bike and try for the interstate.

Then I climbed a small hill and saw Freeze's house in the distance. That vile and ruthless son of a bitch Leather Pants had come through for me after all.

I was about to start toward the house when a pair of hands grabbed me from behind and threw me to the ground.

Chapter Forty-Two

Juliet felt the van slow down. It made a series of turns and then hissed to a stop.

"We're here," Wade said. "I want you to put your hand on my shoulder, same as you did when we left your room. I'm going to lead you to your house, where you'll be staying for the duration of the game."

"OK," Juliet said.

They disembarked and she kept her hand on Wade's shoulder. They started out on pavement, moved to what felt like a trail lined with pine needles, and finally walked into some fairly heavy underbrush. They trudged through the thickets and thistles at a lazy pace for maybe ten minutes. In and out of the shadows. Juliet figured they traveled half a mile or so east of the beaten path. She knew it was east because the sun was directly in front of them.

"You can take your blindfold off now," Wade said.

Juliet took her blindfold off, saw a tiny wood-frame structure with a brass 9 tacked to the porch.

Wade showed her around, told her best of luck. They shook hands, and she stood on the porch and watched him cross the clearing and disappear into the woods.

She went back into the house, tossed her backpack on the floor, sat on the cot, and waited. A few minutes later the audio on the G-29 earpiece buzzed to life and a voice said, "Hello, Number Nine."

"Hello," Juliet said. "Who's this?"

"You can call me Ray. There's been a change of plans. You're going to have to battle another player today after all."

Juliet's heart skipped a beat. "But why?"

"Because Freeze said so."

"But I don't want to. I'm not ready."

"Sorry, but that's the way it is. There are two boxes under your cot. I want you to pull out the one on your left."

"OK."

This was all happening too fast, but what could she do? If she disobeyed, they would fry her heart with the internal defibrillator.

Juliet did what she had to do. She knelt down and reached under the cot.

Chapter Forty-Three

I'd been captured. There were two of them. One of them had a shotgun. They frisked me and took my weapons and handcuffed me and dragged me down the hill to the house. I heard the click of a knife blade lock into place, and one of them started cutting my shirt while another undid my pants. They forced me to the ground and yanked my boots and socks and pants and under-wear off, and the next thing I felt was the stinging cold spray of a garden hose.

"Stand him up."

They stood me up and rinsed me off some more with the icy water.

They patted me down with towels and led me naked through the French doors on the side of the house. Same as the first day I'd been abducted. Déjà vu. The doors led to the fancy gardening shed with all the tools and the wire dog kennel. They forced me into the cage and secured the door with a padlock. The steel wire was very uncomfortable against my naked skin.

The cage didn't smell like bleach this time. It smelled dirty, like sweat and blood.

They wheeled me through the interior set of French doors and down the short hallway to the elevator. We went up and got out on the first floor. "You've Got a Friend" played softly from invisible speakers. The James Taylor version. We turned a couple of corners and entered the large auditorium with the raised platform on the end farthest from the door. Freeze's theater of doom. The same multicolored lights were attached to the same overhead steel trusses, and at the center of the platform Freeze once again sat on his throne. He was still bald and tall and enormously fat. The two large video screens behind him were blank at the moment.

"Leave us alone," Freeze said.

The guys who had wheeled me in left and closed the doors behind them.

"I want to see my wife," I said. "I know she's here somewhere."

Freeze paced the stage. Again the lighting was such that I couldn't make out the features on his face. I knew he was tall and fat, but I couldn't have picked him out of a police lineup or a book of photos if my life depended on it.

"I want to see my wife," I said again. "You hear me, motherfucker?"

"That is *so* not going to happen," Freeze said. "No, you'll never see her again. I'm one hundred percent positive about that. What I'm not one hundred percent positive about is exactly what to do with you now. You've been a bad, bad boy, Number Eight. You have totally fucked up my game. You've totally fucked it up, but I'm thinking maybe I can turn it around and make it the most dramatic conclusion ever. That's what I've been thinking about for the last thirty minutes or so, while most of my people have been rushing around tending to the little mess you left us over in section seven. Let me ask you something: are you familiar at all with the Snuff Tag Nine video game?"

I didn't care about the stupid video game or Freeze's plans for a dramatic conclusion. I wanted to know about my wife.

"Why are you so sure I'm never going to see Juliet again?" I said. "What have you done with her?"

Freeze looked at his watch. "She's on her way to battle Number Seven as we speak. You know, the former Navy SEAL? Hell, she might be there already. I'm not able to watch it live because I have to deal with you. But I'll see the video later. I'm sure it will be spectacular."

"He'll slaughter her," I said. "She doesn't stand a chance, and you know it. Get on the G-twenty-nine and call it off. Call it off and I'll take on Number Seven. I'll give you a good show."

"Oh, you're going to give me a good show anyway. Again, are you familiar with the Snuff Tag Nine video game?"

"Call Juliet's battle off and I'll cooperate. I'll do whatever you want. Otherwise no dice."

"You seem to be forgetting, again, that we know exactly where your daughter is. Would you like to see her thrown into the game as well? It wouldn't take more than a couple of hours for us to—"

"All right," I said. "All right. I read a little bit about Snuff Tag Nine when Nathan Broadway first hired me. Otherwise, no, I'm not familiar with it. The only thing I know about video games is that they exist and that some of them give my daughter a headache when she plays them."

"Snuff Tag Nine is the greatest video game of all time," Freeze said. "And I'm one of the world's best players. Even so, I've never made it to the final level. I've never made it to level twenty. Nobody has. Some of us wonder if level twenty even exists. For years there have been rumors that it's only a myth."

"Level twenty is where the player gets to battle against the game master," I said. "The character named Freeze. The insane billionaire who kidnaps ordinary people and forces them to fight to the death for his own amusement. The character you modeled yourself after."

"That's exactly right," Freeze said. "That's the myth, anyway. Like I said, nobody has ever made it to level twenty in the video game. No player on the planet has ever gotten to battle Freeze. So that's why I've decided to make you the first, Number Eight."

"You want me to fight you?"

"That's the idea."

"Why me?" I said. "Why not wait and see who wins the game. Seems like that would be more—"

"I've been fascinated with you from the beginning, Number Eight. And even more so since I've seen you in action for a few days. You're not especially intelligent, and you're not as strong physically as some of the others, but you have something. Some sort of X factor I can't quite put my finger on. In addition to all that, I would truly like to watch you die in person. You've screwed up my game more than once, and now you've started a fire that could absolutely ruin everything I've worked so hard to build. You're the one I want for level twenty, Number Eight, because I hate you with a passion. I figured you would jump at the chance to fight me."

"I would, if I thought it was going to be a fair fight. But I'm sure you'll have a few of your goons hanging around ready to take me out if it looks like I'm even close to winning."

"Nope. Just me and you and the cameras, right here on this stage. One hour, Number Eight. I'll see you back here in one hour."

Freeze punched some numbers into his cell phone, and the guys came back and wheeled me out. They took me up to my old room. There was a fresh uniform on the bed and a new pair of boots on the floor. The guy with the shotgun stood guard while I took a shower. When I got out, the other guy was standing there with the weapons cart.

"You get to choose again," he said.

"Why can't I just have my old weapons back?" I said.

"That's not the way Freeze wants it."

I wondered if Freeze took a random chance at the weapons he got. I doubted it. He probably handpicked the ones he wanted. So no matter what he said, it wasn't going to be a fair battle. It was rigged to give him the upper hand. Of course it was. He wasn't going to give me a chance to beat him. No way. And I doubted all ten weapons were even on the cart. He probably only loaded the ones he wanted me to have.

I chose drawers number two and seven. The guy opened them and handed me the contents. I got the slingshot and the nightstick. The slingshot was worthless, because we were going to be indoors and there wouldn't be any rocks or anything to use as ammunition. So I basically had a plain old policeman's nightstick to use against whatever Freeze had chosen.

The guy with the shotgun looked at his watch. "Time to go back down," he said.

We went back down. Other than the guys escorting me, the house appeared to be deserted. I hadn't seen anyone else since they'd captured me. Apparently everyone was in section seven trying to extinguish the fire.

They led me to the theater, all the way to the stage this time. We climbed a set of stairs on the right side of the platform, and they took me to a room the size of a walk-in closet. There was a padded chair and a vanity with a sink and a faucet and a lighted mirror.

"Wait here until Freeze calls you on the G-twenty-nine," the guy with the shotgun said. He and his buddy left the room.

I tried sitting in the chair for a few minutes, but I was too restless. I got up and paced back and forth, from one end of the tiny space to the other. It was four steps each way, eight steps round trip. I felt like a tiger in a cage.

I was almost certain Juliet was dead by now, and there was every reason to believe I would be following her soon. At least

I hadn't been forced to watch her die, as I had Joe Crawford. At least I had been spared from that particular horror. Still, I felt responsible for her being roped into this mess. If it weren't for me, Juliet would be safe at home right now, and so would Joe.

I paced around for a few more minutes, feeling anxious and sorry for myself, and then I remembered a quote I read one time on the Internet: *Winners don't blame. Winners don't whine. Winners keep at it until they win.* I didn't remember who the quote was attributed to, but it had struck me as being true when I read it. And it struck me as being true now.

I decided not to give up, even though I knew I was going to die. I decided to go out a winner, giving it my all.

I faced the mirror. I looked haggard. I'd lost weight. My cheeks were sunken, and there were dark circles under my eyes. I looked to be in general poor health, although considering the circumstances and everything I'd been through, I really didn't feel that bad. A nervous energy coursed through me, an angry state of hyperarousal similar to the first few hours of narcotics withdrawal. I felt strong and pissed off, the way you need to feel before beating a fat asshole billionaire sadist to death with a club.

On each side of the mirror were eight light bulbs lined up in a vertical row. They were round and smallish, the actual bulb parts about the size of golf balls. Together they made a nice bright light that would have been sufficient for applying stage makeup or performing brain surgery. I pulled some tissues from the dispenser on the countertop and unscrewed two from each side. I allowed them to cool for a minute and then stuffed them into the left side flap pocket of my black fatigue pants.

I was looking around for a way to short out one of the vacant light sockets and maybe start another fire when Freeze's voice came over the G-29: "Time to play, Number Eight. I'm waiting for you."

I took a deep breath and walked out to the stage.

Chapter Forty-Four

The stage was much larger than it had appeared from my previous perspective. I'd played guitar for Chubby Checker at the 1988 Super Bowl halftime show, and Freeze's stage was about the same size as that one had been. It was huge. You could have parked three tractor-trailers on it side by side. All the lights were on, the overheads and the footlights, and two big spots beamed from trusses below the balconies. It was showtime, ladies and gentlemen.

A dramatic overture faded in from the PA monitors positioned at the edge of the proscenium. I recognized the music. It was "Funeral for a Friend," the orchestral prelude to "Love Lies Bleeding" on Elton John's *Goodbye Yellow Brick Road* album. It was Freeze's way of taking a prebattle stab at me, of reminding me of Joe and Juliet, of fucking with my head and trying to distract me from the task at hand. I tried to ignore it. What I couldn't ignore, though, was the imposing and altogether theatrical figure that now emerged from behind a curtain twenty feet to my left. It was Freeze, all six foot seven and four hundred pounds of him, dressed in a shiny satiny costume complete with puffy sleeves and a pointy hat and curly-toed slippers. The fabric was purple, dotted with glittery white images of moons and stars, and the shoes were studded with multicolored rhinestones. His face had been painted white, with yellow stars outlining his eye sockets and a black frown outlining his mouth. *We're off to see the wizard, the wonderful wizard of hell.*

The article I'd read about the Snuff Tag 9 video game hadn't mentioned anything about costumes and makeup. This was just some of Freeze's dramatic lunacy. His own embellishments. He held a wand, but there was nothing magic about it. It was the stun baton, waiting to discharge over half a million volts of electricity into my body.

"Hello, Number Eight. So nice of you to join me. Do you like the music I chose? Are you familiar with it?"

"I owned it before you were born," I said.

"Good. Now listen, because this is very important. Weapons are not allowed until you hear the intro to 'Love Lies Bleeding.' Understand?"

"What are we going to do until then? Wrestle? I don't think so. You outweigh me by over two hundred pounds."

"My game, my rules. If you refuse to engage, your daughter will suffer the consequences."

He wasn't even going to give me the chance to use my measly weapons. He wanted to kill me with his bare hands. He skipped toward me, doing little twirls on the way, like some sort of dancing hippopotamus. I stood my ground until he got to within a few feet of me, and then I dropped to the floor and rolled toward his legs. Not the smartest move in the world, considering I had lightbulbs in my pocket. The crushed glass from at least one of them ground painfully into my thigh, and a warm trickle of blood followed.

Despite my ill-advised maneuver, I caught Freeze just below the left knee with my right arm and shoulder, and he stumbled and tripped and landed belly down. He almost landed on top of me. I had to roll out of the way quickly. If he had landed on top of me, that would have been it. I would have been crushed and smothered. Maybe it was my imagination, but I thought I felt the whole platform rattle for a second when he went down. Like an aftershock from an earthquake.

I got up and straddled his shoulders, pulled his hat off, and grabbed two handfuls of his greasy hair. I tried to break his neck with a quick upward jerk, but he stiffened and my hands slipped and then he bucked and rolled to the side and I went tumbling like a rodeo cowboy thrown from a bull.

"Thought you had me, didn't you?" Freeze said. He was on his hands and knees looking at me. A thread of slobber dangled from the right side of his grotesquely made-up mouth, glimmering like quicksilver under the hot stage lights. He was smiling. He was enjoying this. It was really like a game to him, as if we were a couple of school chums playing king of the hill.

The massive wizardly form somehow rose to a standing position and stomped toward me. He walked stiff-legged, shambling along with his arms out in front like Frankenstein. He was actually laughing now. I wondered if he had smoked some weed or taken some other drug before coming out to battle me. That's the vibe I got. He seemed high.

I got up and started sidestepping in a circle. I locked in with his eyes, which were big and round and glassy and bloodshot. He lunged for me, those chubby fingers of his aimed at my throat, but I dipped and dodged and managed to throw an uppercut to his solar plexus as I backpedaled stage left. It didn't faze him. He coughed once and kept coming toward me.

If this had been a boxing match, I would have been ahead on points. But that's not how this was going to work. I could have hit him a thousand times, and it wouldn't have mattered. The kill was all that mattered. Winner takes all. I was wearing myself out trying to fight him. I was sweating and huffing and puffing and my legs were like cooked spaghetti. I kept waiting for the bell to ring. I needed to go to my corner. I needed to collapse on my stool and take a breather. I needed for my manager to give me a pep talk. Like Rocky Balboa. Rocky had it easy. Compared to what I was facing, Rocky's battle was a stroll in the park. I wanted to call out for Adrian, only my Adrian was named Juliet and she was probably dead now.

Freeze took two steps toward me, and I took two steps back. "Funeral for a Friend" was almost over. It had been a long time since I'd heard it, but it was ingrained into my memory like the voice of an old pal. I knew it by heart. It was almost over, and once it was, the intro to "Love Lies Bleeding" would start and weapons would be allowed. That's what I was waiting for. No more hand-to-hand with this behemoth. Thirty more seconds, I thought. Thirty more seconds and I would pull the nightstick from my belt loop and charge him. I would charge him and bash his stupid fat head right the fuck in. I gripped the handle and kept sidestepping and backpedaling and waiting.

And then the fog rolled in.

Machines from both sides of the stage erupted with thick rolling clouds, and in a matter of seconds the entire area was engulfed with a multicolored haze. Visibility zero. I couldn't see him, and he couldn't see me. But he could hear me. I was wearing heavy boots, and he was wearing satin rubber-soled slippers. He always made sure he had the advantage in one way or another. One move and he would zero in on me and squash me like a bug. In an effort to level the playing field, I sat down and yanked my boots off and chucked them blindly into the distance. Now I could move around silently, same as him.

"Good move, Number Eight," he said. "Only, now you don't have any shoes. It's going to be hard to beat me without shoes."

He laughed maniacally. His voice seemed to be coming from everywhere. I couldn't track it.

I figured he wouldn't allow the fog machines to run for long. The mist was obstructing the cameras, and I knew he wanted the death scene to be fully visible. My death scene. He wanted his demented audience to see, in vivid detail, the slaughter of the player who had dared to cross him, the player who had made it to level twenty.

The intro to "Love Lies Bleeding" came in, signaling that weapons were allowed.

I pulled my nightstick.

The haze began to clear, and immediately it became obvious why he had fogged the stage in the first place. Kidney-shaped beds of red-hot steaming coals had been dragged in and placed here and there, like sand traps on a golf course. Freeze had anticipated me ditching my shoes. Now my movements were severely limited, limited to where the hotbeds were not. One step out of line and the bottoms of my feet would be seared like burgers on a grill. Things just kept getting worse. I felt like an idiot for taking my shoes off. Freeze was toying with me. He was loving this shit. He was loving watching me sweat.

He tiptoed toward me, walking through the hot coals like nobody's business. There must have been some sort of heatproof barrier between his sparkly twinkly slippers and his feet. With unlimited financial resources, you can pretty much have whatever you want. He could have ordered those gaudy motherfuckers from NASA for all I knew. Maybe the soles had been fashioned from reentry heat tiles off the retired space shuttle or something. Whatever the shoes were made from, they did the trick. He showed no signs of discomfort as he gaily danced toward me, disturbingly graceful and agile for a monster his size.

I figured I had one chance at winning this thing. One in a million. I pulled out my slingshot and loaded it with one of the lightbulbs from the dressing room. I nearly cut a finger off when I reached into my pocket, but I was so amped on adrenaline I didn't even feel it. I stretched the sling to its limit, took aim, and fired. I got lucky. I got luckier than I'd ever gotten in my entire life. The bulb hit him dead center in the forehead and shattered with a pop. It took him by surprise. He hadn't been expecting it. He staggered back a couple of steps. Bright red blood gushed from the wound. I ran toward him with the nightstick raised over my head, as if I were about to serve a tennis ball. I wanted to come down hard on the top of his skull. I wanted to end this thing before he had a chance to regain his composure. I figured his guys were waiting in the wings. I figured they would cut me in half with the shotgun as soon as I delivered the fatal blow, and I was OK with that. I was OK with dying as long as I could take Fat Boy with me.

But Fat Boy had been bluffing. The light bulb to the forehead hadn't really dazed him much at all. When I got to within three feet of him and started to come down with the nightstick, he smiled and shot me in the gut with the stun baton. I froze midstride. Every nerve cell in my body, from the nails on my pinky toes to the hair on my crown, screamed in fiery pain. I stiffened like a plastic mannequin for a brief moment and then fell to the hardwood stage floor with a thud.

I was aware of my surroundings, but I couldn't move. Total paralysis. While Elton John sang about passing through burning hoops of fire, steam rose from the hot coals on both sides of me. Freeze casually walked through them, knelt beside me, and pulled his second weapon, the survival knife.

He gripped the handle with both hands and raised the weapon over his head, ready to plunge it into my heart. He looked me in the eye and said, "Tomorrow, and tomorrow, and tomorrow creeps in this petty pace from day to day to the last syllable of recorded time; and all our yesterdays have lighted fools the way to dusty death. Out, out, brief candle! Life's but a walking shadow, a poor player that struts and frets his hour upon the stage and then is heard no more. It is a tale told by an idiot, full of sound and fury, signifying—"

Before he could say *nothing* and bury the dagger in my chest, a deafening blast rang out and the side of his head exploded and showered me with blood and bone and brain tissue. He fell sideways and landed in the hot coals to my left. The stench of rayon melting onto his skin mingled with the smoky aroma of charred flesh. I couldn't hear anything, but the effects from the stun baton were wearing off. I started to get some feeling back in my arms and legs.

I felt as though I had been granted some sort of pardon, but I didn't want to celebrate too soon. I didn't know what was coming next.

I tried to get up but could only manage a partial sitting position. I thought maybe one of the stooges who had captured me had come to his senses and taken Freeze out.

But that's not what happened.

I looked to the edge of the stage, and Juliet was standing there with the Walther 9mm semiautomatic pistol I'd left under her bed.

Chapter Forty-Five

The emergency room nurse said I looked emancipated.

She meant *emaciated*.

"That's right," I said. "I might be skinny, but at least I'm free."

She gave me a puzzled look. She didn't get it.

I chalked it up to fatigue. Hers, not mine. The ER was short-staffed. She had worked all night and was working over into the day shift for a few hours to help. That's dedication. Nurses had an extremely difficult job sometimes.

I was married to one, so I knew.

I got a chance to talk to Juliet for a few minutes before the ambulances arrived and carted us away from Freeze's hellish playhouse forever. I'd left the pistol from the maintenance guy's car under her bed, along with a note explaining that the defibrillators were phony. Armed with the gun and that bit of knowledge, I figured she might be able to escape before being forced into battle. The odds were still a million to one against her, but she could have made a run for it. She could have tried to save herself.

Instead, she chose to try to save me.

She followed the smoke to the house I'd torched and stayed out of sight until she was able to isolate one of the guys there trying to put the fire out. She threatened to shoot him if he didn't give her directions to Freeze's house. He refused to talk—until she told him about the defibrillators being nothing but inert chunks of stainless steel.

"I'm living proof," she said. "See, I have one too, and I'm way beyond the boundary. If Freeze was telling the truth, I would be dead by now."

Knowing he now had a chance to actually walk out of the swamp alive, the guy she held the gun on gave her the information she needed.

Juliet found her way to the mansion, but then she had to get past the two men Freeze had kept there with him. They weren't expecting anyone, so they'd gotten a little careless. They pulled out the beds of hot coals when the fog machines came on, and while they were doing that Juliet found their shotgun. She held it on them when they returned to the lighting booth, and then she forced them into a supply closet and wedged a chair under the doorknob.

With them out of the way, Freeze was a sitting duck. She used the nine-millimeter pistol I'd left for her because the scattershot pattern of a shotgun blast would have taken me out as well. Smart woman. I was glad I'd taken the time, years ago, to teach her a little about guns.

After killing Freeze, Juliet climbed onto the stage and tended to my bleeding finger. I was on my back, still feeling the effects of the stun baton. She applied a pressure bandage, and then she just sat there beside me for a while, stroking my forehead with her cool fingers. We heard the rotor blades of a helicopter whirring overhead and sirens wailing in the distance. Apparently someone had finally noticed the smoke from the fire I'd started and had alerted the authorities. Help was on the way.

"I love you," I said.

"And I love you, my darling."

"What about my affair in LA?" I said.

She paused for a second and then said, "What affair?"

That's what I needed to hear. She leaned over and kissed me then, and for the first time in a long time I felt like everything was going to be all right.

We rode in separate ambulances to the trauma center in Jacksonville. They wheeled me to a curtained-off area, and I assumed Juliet was taken somewhere nearby. A couple of hours and a couple of liters of IV fluids later, she stepped in and asked me how I was doing.

"How come you get to walk around?" I said.

"I wasn't starved and dehydrated like you," she said. "How do you feel?"

"Surprisingly well, but the doctor wants to admit me for twenty-four-hour observation."

"That's probably a good idea."

I shook my head. "It's a terrible idea."

"Why?"

"Because we have a ball game to go to, that's why."

It took some coaxing, but Juliet finally agreed to call Brittney and have her pick us up at the hospital. I signed out against medical advice, and we drove straight over to the stadium to watch the Florida Gators play the Georgia Bulldogs.

I knew there would be a lot of things to clear up regarding the whole Snuff Tag 9 thing. Detectives from the Jacksonville Sheriff's Office had spoken with us at the hospital. They were satisfied that we had been taken against our will and that everything we'd done was in self-defense. Still, they told us to not leave the area for the next few weeks. There would be a major investigation, they said, by local authorities and by the feds.

And there was.

In the weeks to come, we would learn more about everything that had happened, and we would learn some astonishing details about the man who called himself Freeze. His real name was Malden Zephauser, for instance, and his father had first made a fortune in oil and then in technology. When Daddy died of a heart attack at the age of fifty-four, young Malden had inherited over twenty billion dollars.

With that much money, you can do anything you want. You can submarine to the bottom of the sea or rocket to outer space. You can start your own country if you want to. It funded his little playground in the swamp with no problem, and it kept a cartel of career criminals on the payroll.

The guys at the mansion were only the tip of the iceberg. Retail video game outlets had been set up all across the eastern United States, mostly in towns nobody had ever heard of. Towns like Quincy, Illinois, and Bainbridge, Georgia. Malden used the locations to sponsor in-store Snuff Tag 9 tournaments. When someone filled out a form to participate, the manager would forward that information, and Malden would pick the cream of the crop for his real-life version.

So Nathan Broadway had guessed right about that part, about why he'd received the letter in the first place. Someone had gotten his name and address from a card he filled out in a video game store. It was the one thing all the contestants—that is, victims— had in common, and the FBI had never made the connection.

Then I came along.

A pair of agents had interviewed Joe Crawford soon after I disappeared. Joe told them about the letter I was investigating, and from there the feds started putting two and two together. They were actually close to cracking the case, closer than they even knew, but not close enough.

Juliet and I would have died if we hadn't done what we did. Unless of course one of us had won the game, which didn't seem likely. Not with a former Navy SEAL and an ex–Marine Corps airline pilot still playing.

When Number Six and Number Seven heard the helicopters and the sirens, they retreated to their houses and stayed there. A few hours later, a battalion of National Guardsmen who were combing the area found them. Number Three, the radiologist I'd bound and gagged and performed surgery on, survived as well, although rumor had it he'd been confined to a psychiatric ward for further evaluation.

The men who comprised the staff at the mansion were all arrested. It turned out that some of them were winners from previous years. Their actual prize was a lifetime of servitude, not the opulent existence in a foreign country they had been promised. They all had defibrillators implanted in their chests, which they thought made escape impossible. Those guys were eventually released. Some of them landed book deals and others became the subjects of heartwarming reunion shows.

The films Malden Zephauser produced were distributed via e-mail, mostly to wealthy clients overseas, and although their content called for the utmost discretion, some of the footage had started showing up on rogue websites. One of the videos actually went viral. I couldn't understand that kind of mindset. Anyone who took pleasure in watching men slaughter each other needed to get a life.

We learned all that, but the thing I was most curious about remained a mystery. Who were The Sexy Bastards? Nobody seemed to have a clue. Maybe the term was a code name for something. Maybe it was a secret society of billionaires aiming to rule the world.

Or maybe The Sexy Bastards were a figment of Malden Zephauser's imagination. He'd said nobody would ever know their identities, and so far he was right.

I knew there would be court dates and police station interviews and further medical treatment and maybe some therapy sessions for post-traumatic stress syndrome. There would be surgery consults to remove the fake defibrillators, and of course the media would be yapping about the whole ordeal for months.

All that would happen, but not today. Today was for football.

It was a crisp, cool October Saturday, with just enough breeze to keep the flags waving. We were in the middle tier, near the end zone on the Florida side, not the best seats but not the worst. I had a hot dog and a beer and the two best women in the world at my side.

I was in heaven, and I hoped it would never end.

Acknowledgments

The publication of another novel is always a celebration for me. Though the actual writing process is by nature solitary, turning a manuscript into a book is always a collaborative effort. In no particular order, these are some of the people who have helped me along the way. Please forgive me if I have forgotten anyone.

Thanks to all the wonderful folks at Thomas and Mercer, and their associates, especially Andy Bartlett, Charlotte Herscher, Renee Johnson, and Jacque Ben-Zekry. I know that you truly care about the books you release to the world, and it shows.

Thanks to my agents, Jane and Miriam, for being such great first readers and business partners. I consider myself truly fortunate to have Dystel and Goderich Literary Management as part of my team.

Thanks to all my friends, family members, and peers, for their continuing support. Corey Hardin, Kathy Ledford, Sue Mudd, Stephen Parrish, Erica Orloff, Joe Konrath, Mark Terry, Jon VanZile, Dan Peters, Kathy Blue Quindoza, David Ryan, Scott Nicholson, David Morrell, Lee Goldberg, Bill Rabkin, Melody

Woods Raymond, Nita Bingham, Norm Kelly, Mike Priddy, Alan Orloff, Jane Driskell, Allison Brennan, Blake Crouch, Bud Elder, Char Chaffin, Dana King, Denise Puthuff, Eric Christopherson, Dusty Rhoades, LaDonna Koebel, Lainey Bancroft, Linda McCandless, Tess Gerritsen, Tammy Downard, Trish Barr Johns, Pete Helow...and so many more. At one time or another, every one of you has touched my life in amazing ways, and the ongoing journey would not be the same without you.

And a very special thanks to Bob Florence, my best friend since sixth grade, for helping me with the explosive ordnance disposal work in *Crosscut*. Your expertise is much appreciated, my brother.

About the Author

Photo by Pete Helow, 2011

Jude Hardin is coauthor of the Dead Man series of adventure/horror thrillers created by Lee Goldberg and William Rabkin. His debut novel featuring Nicholas Colt—*Pocket-47*—received a starred review from *Publishers Weekly*. *The New York Times* best-selling author Tess Gerritsen wrote, "*Pocket-47* sucked me in and held me enthralled…[Nicholas Colt] is a character I'm eager to follow." And David Morrell, creator of *Rambo*, called the second Nicholas Colt thriller, *Crosscut*, "fast, fierce, and relentless." Hardin has held down a variety of jobs—from drummer to chemical plant supervisor to freelance journalist—each of which fuels his writing. When he isn't creating his next story, he enjoys fishing with his son. He lives in north Florida.

Made in the USA
Charleston, SC
09 November 2012